TENMILE

TENMILE

By *NEW YORK TIMES* BESTSELLING AUTHOR

SANDRA DALLAS

PUBLISHED *by* SLEEPING BEAR PRESS™

Text copyright © 2022 Sandra Dallas
Cover illustration copyright © 2022 Jenny Zemanek

Sleeping Bear Press™

2395 South Huron Parkway, Suite 200, Ann Arbor, MI 48104
www.sleepingbearpress.com
© Sleeping Bear Press

Printed and bound in China.
10 9 8 7 6 5 4 3 2 1

Library of Congress Cataloging-in-Publication Data
Names: Dallas, Sandra, author.
Title: Tenmile / Sandra Dallas.
Description: Ann Arbor, MI : Sleeping Bear Press, [2022] | Audience: Ages
9-11. | Audience: Grades 4-6. | Summary: A thirteen-year-old girl living
in an 1880 Colorado gold-mining town witnesses the hardships of her
community as she assists her father, the town doctor.
Identifiers: LCCN 2022003622 | ISBN 9781534111622 (hardcover)
Subjects: CYAC: City and town life--Fiction. | Fathers and
daughters--Fiction. | Medical care--Fiction. | Colorado--History--19th
century--Fiction. | LCGFT: Historical fiction. | Novels.
Classification: LCC PZ7.D1644 Te 2022 | DDC [Fic]--dc23
LC record available at https://lccn.loc.gov/2022003622

To Forrest, from Sissy

1

THE BABY STRETCHED ITS ARMS and legs as Sissy wrapped it in the soft flannel blanket. She smiled at the wriggling infant with its tiny wrinkled face.

"Boy or girl?" Greenie asked.

"Girl." The two stood in the kitchen. Sissy had come to fetch the blanket.

Greenie nodded her approval. "That will make her mother happy. Three boys and at last a girl."

"I don't think Mrs. Burke knows yet. She was too groggy."

"What did Mr. Burke say?"

"He's outside. He was so nervous that Papa wouldn't let

him stay in the surgery any longer."

"Is she all right?"

Sissy nodded. "Papa says so. Isn't she sweet, Greenie?"

"Sweet as you were when you were born." She smiled at Sissy. "Doc must be glad you were there to help, Sissy."

Sissy looked down at the infant, who made mewling sounds. The baby's tiny pink tongue popped in and out of her mouth. Sissy picked up another blanket from the pile that had been set beside the cookstove to warm. Despite the heat from the fire in the stove, the room was chilly, and Sissy wanted to keep the infant protected.

She went to the window and looked out. The sun had reached the tips of the mountain peaks. It made the snow gleam a blinding white. The sky was lit with the fire of sunrise. Gold edged the red streaks. "Look, baby. Look at the sky. It's your birthday present," Sissy said.

"Sis!" Doc called. "Are you dawdling?"

"No, sir," Sissy replied as Doc came into the kitchen. "I'm taking care of the baby. Then I'm going to school. The Burke boys will want to know the baby has arrived and that she's a girl."

Doc frowned at her. "It's not your place to tell them.

What happens in the surgery is nobody's business. I've told you that before. Everything there is private. We never discuss a patient with anyone."

"No, sir," Sissy said. It stung that Doc had scolded her. She hadn't meant anything by it.

"I was just showing the baby to Greenie," she said.

"I believe Mrs. Burke would rather you bring her the baby," Doc said. "She's awake now."

Greenie gave Sissy a sympathetic look when Sissy glanced at her. The girl followed Doc back into the surgery, where Mrs. Burke was resting. Doc's office and surgery were connected to the house. The surgery was the room where Doc treated patients. He examined people, set broken bones, and performed operations there. That morning, he had delivered the Burke baby in that room.

"Let Mrs. Burke see her baby," Doc said.

"Yes, sir." Sissy held up the baby.

"Is it a girl?" Mrs. Burke asked.

Sissy looked at Doc. He was always the one who told a new mother the sex of her child.

This time, however, Doc said, "Well, answer her."

"A girl," Sissy said.

Mrs. Burke smiled and reached for the infant. "The boys will be at school by now. I hope you'll let them know they have a sister."

Sissy would get to tell them after all. She hid a smile and didn't look at Doc.

"I hope she grows up to be as helpful as you," Mrs. Burke continued.

I hope I won't be here to see it, Sissy thought. *I hope I'll be a long way from here by then.*

Later, when both Mrs. Burke and the baby were resting, Doc came into the kitchen. Sissy had eaten breakfast and was gathering her schoolbooks. "I'll get your breakfast, Doc," Greenie said.

"Yes, of course," Doc replied. As he sat down at the table, he reached into his pocket and took out a handful of heavy silver dollars. "Mr. Burke paid me when I went outside to tell him about the baby. Then he left for the mine. You'd think the Yellowcat would let a man have a day off when his wife has a baby, but it doesn't." He jiggled the coins.

"How much?" Sissy asked.

"Three dollars."

Sissy grinned. "That means he asked the right question."

Doc nodded. Sissy knew he charged four dollars for a delivery if the father's first question after the baby was born was about its sex. But he charged only three dollars if the man first asked if his wife was all right.

Doc set the coins on the table and lined them up. Then he picked up the shiniest one and handed it to Sissy. "I think my helper deserves one of these. You can buy something for yourself, maybe a nice doll."

Sissy thanked her father and took the dollar to her bedroom. Greenie followed Sissy into her room. "You're not going to buy a doll, are you?" she asked.

Sissy shook her head. "Does Papa really think I still play with dolls?"

"You're going to put it in the tin can, right?" Greenie asked.

"Of course," Sissy said.

Greenie nodded her approval. It was a secret the two of them shared. The can held nearly fifty dollars in coins Doc had given her over the years for helping with his work.

"You're still saving the money for college, aren't you?"

Sissy nodded. She wasn't sure what she would study in college or what she would do after she graduated. But she knew college meant she could leave Tenmile, the smoky, noisy mining town where she'd lived for all thirteen years of her life.

2

Sɪssʏ ᴋɴᴇᴡ sʜᴇ ᴡᴏᴜʟᴅ ʙᴇ ʟᴀᴛᴇ. The final bell in the steeple on top of the school had already rung. The teacher would be annoyed. Still, Sissy smiled to herself as she hurried along the road to the schoolhouse, humming a little song. She didn't care what the teacher said. She thought of the tiny infant she had held that morning. The baby was so dear. When Sissy had handed her to her mother, the infant's face was puckered, and her eyes had shut tight as she'd let out a loud cry. Clumps of pale hair stuck out all over her head, and the sight had made Sissy laugh.

The Burkes were proud of their new baby, but Sissy

couldn't help but wonder about the little girl's future. She would grow up in Chicken Flats, a rough settlement of shacks in the center of town, home to the Irish and Russians, the Finns and Mexicans and Cornish. Like Mr. Burke, all the men worked in the mines and the mill. Adjacent to Chicken Flats was the downtown area with stores and saloons, restaurants and gambling halls. Tenmile was in a valley completely surrounded by the mountains of the Tenmile Range. The Yellowcat Mine was on the mountain to the north, high above Chicken Flats. Sissy lived in a nicer area on the eastern mountain slope while the mine owner and other wealthy people were on the southern slope.

"She's number forty," Doc had said as he looked at the baby with pride. "Delivering babies just might be the greatest pleasure of being a physician. Did you know I've delivered forty babies here in Tenmile?"

Sissy hadn't helped with all of them, of course. Doc had been a doctor since before she was born. *One of the forty was me*, she thought as she walked along. Still, she had helped with several births. She loved seeing new life, but she thought again about how difficult things would be for a little girl growing up in Chicken Flats.

Class had started by the time Sissy arrived at school. Miss Braddock, the teacher, was writing the date on the blackboard: Wednesday, March 24, 1880.

She stopped when Sissy entered the room. "Well, it's nice you could join us while it's still the twenty-fourth, Sallyann," Miss Braddock said. Sallyann was Sissy's real name, but only her teacher called her that.

"I'm sorry," Sissy said. "You see—"

"No excuses," Miss Braddock interrupted. "Everyone else managed to be here on time. I don't know why you couldn't."

"I was helping Doc deliver a baby," Sissy said before Miss Braddock could stop her.

"Oh," the teacher said. "I suppose that's different."

The girls in the class smiled. "Oh, a baby!" Sissy's friend Martha Popov exclaimed.

"Isn't that sweet!" Nelle Ridge, another friend, said. "You got to be there? You're so lucky."

"I helped the midwife who delivered my last brother because Doc was away," Martha said.

Life was hard in gold mining towns like Tenmile. Sissy knew a baby brought joy because it was new life. Doc had delivered many of her classmates—some at home, some in his surgery—but not all of them. If Doc was away or a woman couldn't afford a doctor, she sent for a neighbor or for the midwife who lived over the mountain in Swandyke. She might pay the midwife with a bucket of coal or a bushel of potatoes. Those babies were delivered at home, so most girls knew about childbirth.

"I wish my mother would have another baby, even though it'll mean a lot more work for me," Martha added. "Last time, I had to be away from school for a month helping her."

"Lucky!" one of the boys said in a loud voice.

Sissy waited until the talk settled down. Then she announced, "I helped Doc deliver Jack Burke's sister!" Sissy turned to grin at Jack.

"*Sister!* No foolin'! We got us a girl!" Jack shouted. "Thanks, Sissy," he added, as if Sissy were responsible.

"You can come see her in the surgery after school. Your ma'll be there till your dad gets off shift. Then Doc will take them home in our buggy."

"What'd she name her?" Jack asked.

"She didn't yet. Your ma said she was sure it would be another boy, so she didn't have a girl's name picked out."

"Yeah, she was going to call him Hubert. I hope she doesn't use that for our sister. I better tell my brothers." Jack stood up and headed for the door.

"That can wait until recess," Miss Braddock said.

"No, it can't!" Jack told her. "We waited six years for a girl. They're not waiting any longer."

"Let's make a card for Mrs. Burke. We can all sign it," Martha suggested.

Miss Braddock had been about to start a spelling lesson. She sighed and glanced down at the little watch pinned to her dress. "I hope there won't be any more babies born today, Sissy. We have lessons to do."

"No, ma'am. I'm pretty sure of it," Sissy said. She wasn't completely sure, though. Who knew when a baby might arrive?

Jack walked home from school with Sissy. His younger brothers ran ahead of them. Their dinner buckets banged against their legs.

"I want to come, too, so I can see the baby," Nelle said.

"Me too," Martha added.

"You can't," Sissy said.

"Why not?" Nelle asked.

"Only family. Doc's orders," Sissy said, feeling important.

"Jack, where'd Ma get that baby?" Little Joe called over his shoulder. At six, he was the youngest Burke boy.

"From Doc Carlson," Jack replied.

"Where'd Doc get it?"

Jack considered the question, then winked at Sissy. "I don't know. Maybe he found her on a mine dump."

Little Joe thought that over. "Let's ask him where. Maybe there's more of them out there. We can sell them."

Jack and Sissy laughed. Along with Martha and Nelle, Jack was one of Sissy's best friends. They'd gone to school together their whole lives, and both planned to graduate from high school and go to college.

Jack hoped to be an engineer. He'd once told Sissy, "I don't want to go down in the hole with a pick. I'm not going to work a shift like Pa. There's never enough money, and we're always worried he'll get hurt." If Mr. Burke got injured and couldn't work, Jack would have to quit school to go into the mine.

"I hope you make it. There aren't a lot of boys who graduate from high school in Tenmile. Shoot, most don't even finish eighth grade," Sissy had said.

"I know. They go underground at the Yellowcat or one of the smaller mines to help out their families. But I'm luckier than they are. Pa wants me to go to college. He wants better for me."

Now, as he hurried behind his brothers to Sissy's house, Jack said, "You know, Pa says if I graduate, I could get a job that pays good. Then I could help my brothers go to college, too."

"What about your new sister?"

"Girls don't go to college. They just get married," he said.

Sissy elbowed him. "Take that back."

"Oh, I don't mean you. You're different."

"You mean I'm weird."

"Yeah, but in a good way. What would you do if you went to college? You couldn't be an engineer."

The two of them stepped aside to let an ore wagon pass. "I don't know, but something that'll get me out of Tenmile. I'm tired of this town."

"You can say that again."

❦

The younger boys had reached the Carlson house and were hopping from one foot to the other as they waited for Jack and Sissy to catch up. When she reached them, Sissy put her finger to her lips. "Be very quiet. Your mother may be sleeping. The baby, too. And don't touch the baby until you wash your hands."

"Aw," Peter said. At nine, he was the middle boy. He looked down at his dirty hands, then held them behind his back.

"You don't want to get your sister dirty, do you?" Sissy asked.

Peter shrugged. "How's she going to keep clean?"

It was a good question. Doc always preached the importance of cleanliness to his patients.

"Washing your hands is the best way of keeping children from getting sick," he told them. The Burke house did not have running water, though. And with three boys and a father who worked underground in a mine, it was hard for Mrs. Burke to keep everything clean. The baby would get dirty soon enough.

Still, Sissy told them, "You can't touch your sister with dirty hands. We'll go into the kitchen, and you can wash up at the pump." Most of the houses in Tenmile got their water from wells or even the creek, but the Carlson house had a pump at the kitchen sink.

"I get to pump the handle!" Little Joe cried. He and his brothers followed Sissy inside. They took turns holding out their hands as Little Joe pumped water over them. Greenie handed the children a towel.

"We got us a sister," Peter said.

"Well, aren't you the lucky ones," Greenie told them. "Your ma's in the spare bedroom that we use for patients. She's awake. You can go see her." She pointed to a door.

Peter started for the room, then stopped and sniffed. "What's that smell?" The kitchen was filled with the scents of ginger and cinnamon.

"It's gingerbread. I always make gingerbread when I know there's little boys coming to meet their sister for the first time."

Little Joe looked at the table, where the warm gingerbread sat in a pan. Then he glanced at the door. "I guess I could eat a piece now."

"You go see your mother first," Greenie said. She shooed the boy away from the table.

Little Joe led his brothers into the room. "We got gingerbread," he announced to his mother. "That lady made it for us."

Mrs. Burke was sitting up in bed. The infant was wrapped in one of the surgery's flannel blankets. The mother looked tired but happy. "I've got something even better than gingerbread," she said. She held up the baby, who was making funny faces. She wrinkled her nose and opened and closed her mouth. The boys rushed to the bedside. They gathered around the little girl and stared at her with awe.

"Is that ours?" Little Joe asked.

His mother nodded.

"Does she want some gingerbread? I'll share mine with her."

"Not yet." Mrs. Burke laughed. "Maybe next week."

Sissy laughed, too.

"She looks like a puppy," Peter said. He reached out a finger and let the tiny girl grab it. Peter grinned. "She likes me, Ma."

"What are we going to name her?" asked Little Joe, who'd

been told to expect a brother or a sister.

"I haven't decided. For now we should call her Sister."

Jack and Peter nodded in approval, but Little Joe frowned. Then his face lit up. "I know. Let's call her Brother!"

3

Doc drove Mrs. Burke and the baby home in his buggy. There wasn't enough room for everybody, so the boys ran behind it.

"Tap 'er light," Greenie called as she waved goodbye, the common phrase folks in the mining towns used to mean "take it easy." Greenie had told Sissy that the phrase was used by the miners when they gently tapped dynamite into holes they had drilled in the mine. If they tapped in the charges too hard, they could explode.

Greenie and Sissy stood outside, watching the buggy disappear down the muddy road.

"I hope Doc takes care through all that snowmelt. It's made the streets slippery," Greenie said. It was dark now, and they could see the lights at the mine and mill on the mountain above Chicken Flats. "But nothing ever seems to stop Doc when folks need him."

Sissy shivered, and Greenie asked, "Are you cold?"

"A little."

"It's always cold in these mountains at night." Greenie rubbed her arms with her hands. "Did Mrs. Burke finally pick a name for the baby?"

"Nancy," Sissy replied. "Mrs. Burke said it was her mother's name."

"I kind of liked Brother."

"Me too." Sissy laughed.

Just then there was a loud noise from the mountain. Both of them looked up. "Is there an accident?" Sissy asked.

"Just a shift change at the mill," Greenie said. The mill was adjacent to the mine and treated the gold ore that came from the Yellowcat.

Greenie sighed. "But I guess mine accidents are never far from my mind. You know how Mr. Greenway died."

Sissy did know. Although she had been an infant when

it had happened, she had heard the story many times over the years. Mr. Greenway had been killed in a rockfall in the Yellowcat just after Sissy's mother had died. Since the Greenways had no children, Doc had convinced the widow to move into his house as a housekeeper and surrogate mother to Sissy. She raised Sissy, cooked, kept a small garden, and tended the house. Dr. Carlson always called the housekeeper by her proper name: Mrs. Greenway. When she was small, however, Sissy hadn't been able to say Greenway and had dubbed the woman Greenie. Greenie didn't mind, and the name had stuck. Sissy loved Greenie. The woman was the only mother she had ever known.

"Doc does a fine job of delivering babies and taking care of sick people, but he sure didn't know much about looking after a little girl back then," Greenie said now.

"You taught me to cook and clean the house." Sissy made a face. She'd never liked doing those things and wasn't very good at them. Then she smiled. "And it was you, not Papa, who gave me the idea that I should go to college one day."

"You have to be prepared. Don't end up like me, a widow with few ways of earning a living. I can barely read

read and write. If your father hadn't taken me in, I'd have ended up in the poorhouse. A woman ought to have a way of supporting herself. Life is hard on the Tenmile."

4

COAL WAS EXPENSIVE. MANY OF the families in Chicken Flats sent their children out with buckets to scavenge for it. They hunted for it on the streets and near the coal yard, but the best place to find it was along the railroad tracks. Coal fueled the train engines, and trains transported coal to the mines and mill in open cars, which meant it often fell and scattered beside the tracks.

One Sunday afternoon in May, several weeks after Nancy Burke was born, Sissy went with Jack and Martha to collect coal for their families. They had invited Nelle to go with them, but Nelle's father, Mr. Ridge, said she had to work at

Delmonico's, their family's restaurant.

"Let's walk along the tracks by the Yellowcat. There's bound to be coal up there," Jack said. He paused and scratched his head. "I wonder who named it the Yellowcat?"

"Louis Humboldt. He's the man who discovered it. He said a yellow cat was sitting on the ore outcropping," Martha answered.

"That figures. Mines get their names for lots of weird reasons," Jack said. "I heard Mr. Humboldt lost the mine in a poker game. Then Mr. Gilpin bought it from the man who won it."

Jack led the way along the tracks, a dented old bucket in his hands. The two girls followed. Martha carried a bucket, too, but not Sissy. Since Doc bought all the coal Greenie used in the cookstove and parlor stove, Sissy didn't need to collect any. She'd give whatever she found to her friends.

A train lumbered along, and Martha yelled, "Hey, mister, throw down some coal!" Sometimes when nobody was looking, a sympathetic railroad worker in an open coal car sent a shovelful of coal over the side. But this man ignored Martha, and she shrugged.

Sissy found a lump of coal lying on the ground and put

it into Martha's pail. Other kids were out picking up coal, too, and Sissy hoped they wouldn't have to fight them for it. A boy named Toby Williams was about to pick up a piece when Donnie Bleeker, an older boy, grabbed it away.

Toby began to cry. Sissy went up to him and put her arm around his shoulders. "It's okay. There's more lumps."

"If I don't get a bucketful, Pa'll whip me," Toby said. The train slowed and stopped, and the railroad worker disappeared. Toby stared at the coal car. "I'm gonna climb up there and throw down some coal. I'll give you half if you pick it up for me."

Sissy gasped. "That's dangerous. If they catch you, you'll get in trouble. Besides, if the train starts again, you could fall and get run over."

"Nobody'll catch me. I'm too fast."

"Don't do it," Sissy said.

"I'll be okay." He handed Sissy his pail.

"Then be careful."

"Aw, don't worry. I know what I'm doing." He stuck out his chest a little and tried to act brave. Still, Sissy knew he was scared.

Toby used the ladder attached to the side of the car to

climb to the top. He picked up a shovel the railroad worker had left and began shoveling chunks of coal over the side. The children nearby rushed to pick it up and add it to their pails.

"That kid's crazy. I'd never do that," Donnie said. There was awe in his voice. But that didn't stop him from grabbing as much coal as he could.

"Remember, half that coal belongs to Toby," Sissy reminded him.

"Yeah, if he can take it away from me."

"Maybe I could, Bleeker," Jack said. He was bigger than Donnie. "Toby's taking a big risk. You owe him."

"Nah, if he's dumb enough—hey, look out!" Donnie yelled.

The kids on the ground stopped what they were doing and looked up at Toby. A railroad worker had climbed on top of the car.

Toby didn't see him. He scooped up a shovelful of coal and was about to throw it down when the man grabbed his arm. "What do you think you're doing up here, kid?" he asked. He was big and brawny. His hands and face were covered with coal dust. Sissy thought he looked scary.

"I ought to throw you off this train. It would serve you right," he said. As he snatched the shovel from Toby, he loosened his grip on the boy.

Toby yanked his arm away and jumped off the coal car, landing hard and rolling onto his side. He got up and began running. The man yelled, "Come on back here, you little thief! I'll teach you to steal coal!"

The man didn't chase Toby, though. He stayed where he was on top of the car, so Sissy thought Toby might be safe. But then she saw another worker climb down from the locomotive and run toward them. The man started after Toby.

"I'll give you the beating of your life!" he yelled.

Toby ran as fast as he could away from the train tracks, toward a road leading to the mine. He kept looking over his shoulder at the railroad worker, not watching where he was going. Just as he reached the road, he stumbled, falling headlong into the path of a wagon driving away from the mine.

The driver saw Toby in the road and pulled back on the horses' reins, but the wagon was heavy, and momentum pushed them forward. Sissy saw Toby put his hands over his head as the horses passed over him. Their hooves missed the boy, but he couldn't escape the heavy wagon wheels. Toby screamed!

The children, pails in hand, ran toward the boy. So did the two railroad workers. Donnie got there first and pulled Toby out of the road. Donnie was crying. "I'd have given him half my coal, really," he said to Sissy.

The railroad men reached them. The man who'd been on top of the car said, "I was just yelling to scare him."

The other said, "I wouldn't have beaten him. I didn't mean it."

The driver had pulled the wagon to a stop, and now he jumped down. "What happened?"

"His legs got crushed," Sissy told him.

"Where's the doctor?"

"My father's the doctor," Sissy said, struggling to catch her breath. "I'll show you where he is."

The driver carefully lifted Toby and placed him in the wagon bed. Toby whimpered and muttered, "My legs . . . my legs hurt awful bad."

"Hurry, get in back with him! I'll ride up front with the driver and tell him the way!" Sissy shouted. She climbed on. Jack, Martha, and Donnie got into the back with Toby.

The driver picked up his whip and lashed the horses, and they raced down the road.

Sissy, still gripping Toby's pail, held on to the seat. She was afraid she would bounce off the wagon. She turned around to see how Toby was doing. Donnie had lifted the boy into his lap so he wouldn't shift around in the wagon. Donnie was still crying. "I shouldn't have took that chunk of coal off him. It's my fault. God's going to punish me."

"He won't do any such thing," Martha said. She held one of Toby's hands and sang a little song to him.

The wagon jolted when the wheels ran over a rock, and Toby cried out.

"Hush, hush," Jack told him. He sounded as if he were talking to his baby sister, Nancy.

"Doc will fix you. He's the best doctor there is. Just hold on," Sissy said. "We'll be there soon."

The wagon had to pass through the center of town before it could head east to Sissy's house. The streets were jammed with prospectors and gamblers. There were housewives going back and forth to the shops. Wagons and carriages clogged the road. The driver swore under his breath.

Farther on, the street was blocked by a delivery wagon

parked halfway into the road. The driver was nowhere in sight. "We'll get him," Jack said.

He and Sissy jumped down and ran into the nearest store. "Move your wagon! A boy's hurt!" she yelled.

"Hold on." A man set down a box and rushed out.

When the street was clear, the driver maneuvered the wagon along it, cracking his whip over the horses' heads. Sissy turned and looked into the wagon bed. Toby had stopped crying.

"Is he passed out?" she asked. Then she put her hand over her mouth. "Is he . . . ?"

"He's not dead," Jack said quickly. He had moved over next to Donnie and was holding Toby's head in his lap. Sissy could see the sweat on Toby's face.

"There!" Sissy pointed to her house. "Around to the side. That's the door to Doc's office." As soon as the wagon stopped, she told Jack, "Keep Toby here until my father can look at him. We have to be careful about moving him." She climbed down from the wagon and ran into Doc's office, dropping the bucket on the doorstep.

Her father looked up as Sissy came in. Her face was dark with coal dust. There were little lines where tears had streaked down through the black.

"What's happened?" Doc asked, rising from his chair.

"It's Toby, a boy from school. A wagon ran over his legs. He's hurt bad, Papa, and I think his legs are broken. He's outside in a wagon."

Doc rushed out the door. He looked down at Toby in the wagon bed, then at Jack and Donnie. "You boys did a good job of holding him still," he said. "Sissy and I will get a stretcher." The two fetched it, and Doc gently lifted the injured boy onto it. Toby whimpered in pain. Then Doc and the driver carried him into the surgery.

The wagon wheels had ripped Toby's pants. Doc cut them off so that he could examine Toby's legs.

"Is it bad?" Sissy asked.

"It's not good." Doc looked around at all the people crowded into the room. The driver had left, but Jack and Donnie and Martha were still there. "We've got too big a crowd in here. Sissy, you stay. You others, go in and ask Mrs. Greenway for something to eat," Doc said.

"Wash your hands, and you might wash your face, too," Doc told Sissy when the three were gone. "The boy's legs aren't crushed, but he may have broken bones. I'll need your help setting them."

As she washed up, Sissy wondered what Doc would want her to do. She'd assisted him lots of times. She'd never helped with a patient with broken bones, though. She was excited but nervous.

Doc worked quietly and efficiently, mumbling to himself as he set the boy's legs. Sissy was used to her father talking that way. It was as if he was explaining to himself what he was doing. She always learned a great deal just by listening.

When Doc was finished, Sissy started gathering the medical instruments they had used to be cleaned and boiled in the kitchen. A sudden pounding on the office door stopped her. Doc sighed. Sissy knew he was tired, but he would never refuse another patient.

"I'll get the door, Papa," Sissy said. She opened it to find a woman with a baby in her arms. Jack was behind them.

"This is Toby's mother, Mrs. Williams," he said. "I went down to Chicken Flats for her. I thought it would be okay."

"Toby's resting in the surgery. I'll fetch Papa."

Mrs. Williams didn't wait. She handed the baby to Sissy and pushed past her into the office. "Where's my boy? Where's Toby?" she wailed.

"In there." Sissy pointed to the surgery, where Doc stood beside Toby.

Mrs. Williams rushed into the room. Sissy and Jack followed. Then Donnie and Martha opened the door between the parlor and the office and stood just outside it.

Doc looked at them and said, "Well, you might as well all come in and see Toby." Then he added, "As you can tell, he came through just fine."

Mrs. Williams began to weep as she went to the operating table and grasped her son's hands. The kids clapped and pounded each other on the back.

"Look, Mother, Doc fixed my legs," Toby told her in a slurred voice.

The woman looked up at Doc, who said, "He won't be able to walk for a while. And he's got to keep the wounds clean. But he should heal just fine. I think it's best if we keep the boy overnight to make sure he doesn't have a setback. He can sleep in the spare room. Sissy and I will keep watch over him. She knows what to do."

Sissy swelled with pride. She was proud of her father and proud that she had helped.

❧

Toby spent the night in the spare bedroom, where Doc could keep an eye on him. Mrs. Williams came early in the morning and sat in the kitchen with Sissy and Greenie while Doc examined her son a final time.

"It's a long walk up this mountain to your house," Mrs. Williams said, when Doc came into the kitchen.

"The high altitude makes walking hard," Doc told her.

Sissy and Greenie exchanged a glance. Doc had told them Toby would be going home that day. They both realized then that the Williamses didn't have a carriage or even a wagon to take Toby home, and he certainly wasn't going to walk. Doc would have to drive him.

"I'll get the buggy," Sissy said.

She went outside to the barn and hitched up the horse. She drove the buggy as close to the door as she could. Then she went into the spare room, where Doc was explaining to Mrs. Williams how to care for Toby.

"I don't know how we can thank you," Mrs. Williams said when Doc was finished. She grabbed his hands. "We don't have no money, but we'll pay you somehow."

"If I hadn't left my coal bucket up by the Yellowcat, I'd pay you with that," Toby said. He laughed, then winced at the pain.

"I think it's outside where I left it," Sissy told him.

"That coal's mighty important. You'll need it to keep warm while you're healing. I think maybe you better keep it," Doc said. "We'll talk about payment later." Sissy knew that meant Doc probably wouldn't charge at all.

Doc carefully picked up Toby, carried him outside, and set him on the buggy seat. Mrs. Williams and Doc crowded in beside him. Doc picked up the reins and was about to slap them on the horse when Sissy said, "Wait, you forgot the coal bucket."

She went to the porch steps, where the bucket was sitting. As she picked it up, she glanced down at it. Toby hadn't had a chance to collect much coal, but the bucket was filled to overflowing. For a moment, Sissy didn't understand. Then she realized that Jack and Donnie and Martha had dumped the coal they had collected into Toby's bucket.

After Doc drove away, Sissy walked up the mountain to a grove of aspen trees she thought of as her own special place. Rock walls surrounded three sides of the space, forming a sort of cove. She could sit in the shelter and look out at the far mountains. The spot was away from the noise and smoke of Tenmile.

Snow had filled the crevices in the rocks, so Sissy sat down on a dead tree that had fallen over. She thought about Toby and how dangerous life was in Tenmile. She thought about the clamor of the mines that never ceased and the foul air that sometimes got so bad she couldn't see across the street in the daytime.

I hate Tenmile! I want to live someplace where a little boy doesn't have to choose between a whipping and risking his life. I can't wait to leave.

5

Sissy was sitting with Jack on the porch of her house when Nelle Ridge showed up. She was puffing from the long climb and sat down on the steps. Nelle was one of Sissy's oldest friends. Sissy couldn't remember a time when they hadn't known each other.

When she'd caught her breath, Nelle said, "I need your help."

"What's up?" Sissy asked.

"I need you to help me make a skirt for Essie for her birthday on Saturday. I don't know how to sew."

"I don't either," Sissy said.

"Me neither," Jack added, and all three of them laughed.

"Oh dear." Nelle took a deep breath. "My sister turns ten on Saturday, and I don't know what to give her. I want it to be something special, because Essie hasn't had a birthday celebration since Ma died."

Mrs. Ridge had passed away two years before. Sissy knew that while Mr. Ridge was German, Mrs. Ridge had been a "Cousin Jenny," as the Cornish women were called. Doc said the Cornish men—"Cousin Jacks"—were in great demand in Tenmile and other gold and silver towns because they were the best at timbering the mines. Sissy remembered how Mrs. Ridge had always made birthdays special for her daughters with her Cornish currant cake.

Essie was a sweet, quiet child who kept to herself. Knowing how much Essie missed her mother, Sissy was eager to help Nelle.

"How about a doll? Girls always like dolls. You like them, don't you?" Jack said. He gave Sissy a sly look.

Sissy poked him with her elbow. "Not anymore."

"I can't afford a doll. I don't have any money," Nelle said. She put her elbows on her knees and held her head in her hands, thinking.

Sissy thought that was odd. Nelle worked at her father's café, where diners left her tips. Sissy wondered what happened to those tips. Maybe, like Sissy, Nelle was saving up to pay for college. She'd often talked about being a teacher.

But since her mother had passed away, Nelle hadn't said anything more about teaching.

Sissy couldn't recall Mr. Ridge ever talking about a career for Nelle either. Perhaps, like a lot of fathers Sissy knew, he didn't approve of education for girls.

"Let's think. I bet there's something you could give her that wouldn't cost money," Jack said. "How about you draw her a picture?"

"A picture of your mother," Sissy added.

"I can't draw any better than I can sew," Nelle told them.

"We can't either," Sissy admitted. Then she suggested, "What if we catch a squirrel? Jack could build a cage for it."

"I could do that," Jack said.

"Wild things die when you put them in cages," Nelle told them.

"I guess that was a pretty stupid idea. I wouldn't like to cage a wild animal, anyway," Sissy said.

"We could pick her a bouquet of wildflowers," Jack said.

"That's a good idea," Sissy said.

"But Essie and I pick them every week for Delmonico's," Nelle told them.

"Then maybe we're going to have to just sing 'Happy Birthday' to her," Jack said.

Sissy jumped up. "That's it! Jack, you're a genius. Essie works Saturdays. We can give her a cake with ten candles, and everybody in the restaurant can sing 'Happy Birthday' to her. What do you think, Nelle?"

Nelle considered that. "It's a wonderful idea. Essie will be thrilled that people care about her birthday. It'll be a surprise. Come on, let's go ask my pa. He hasn't gone to the restaurant yet."

The three trooped down the mountainside to Nelle's home. Her house was nicer than some of the shacks in Chicken Flats. It was built better, and the yard was filled with flowers Mrs. Ridge had planted. Mr. Ridge insisted that the house be as tidy as the restaurant. There were curtains in the windows that Nelle had starched and ironed. The stove was blackened, and a stack of kindling rested in a bucket beside it. The floor was swept, and on the tables were snowy-white doilies Mrs. Ridge had crocheted.

"I forgot Essie was here," Nelle said when the three reached the house.

"I'll keep her busy," Jack said.

While Jack went indoors to talk to Essie, Nelle and Sissy went to the backyard where Mr. Ridge was sitting in an old chair, his feet up on a log. He looked like he was sleeping.

Sissy liked Mr. Ridge. He often brought home leftover pie or cake from Delmonico's, so there were always treats at the Ridge house when she visited. He was a jolly man who teased her about how pretty she was, although Sissy thought she wasn't really. She was too tall and bony, and her hair never seemed to curl, even when Greenie washed it and rolled it up with socks. Still, she was flattered by his compliments.

Sissy noticed that Nelle didn't seem fond of her father, though. Maybe that was because he expected so much from her. Nelle and Essie kept up the house, did the laundry, and worked at the restaurant on Saturdays and Sundays. But that wasn't unusual in Tenmile. Many of Sissy's friends worked to help out their families. Some even dropped out of school to do so. Greenie was right—life was hard for Tenmile people.

"Pa," Nelle said so quietly that Sissy wondered if she was

afraid of waking her father.

"What is it?" he barked. He opened his eyes, but when he saw Sissy, he grinned. "Well, what a nice surprise."

"Hi, Mr. Ridge," Sissy said.

"You get prettier every day," he told her.

Sissy blushed.

"We have something we want to ask you. We need your permission," Nelle said.

Mr. Ridge put his feet down. "What is it?" he asked gruffly.

Sissy wondered if he might tell Nelle no. So before Nelle could ask his permission, Sissy spoke up. "We were thinking it would be fun to have a surprise birthday party for Essie at your restaurant."

"When's her birthday?" Mr. Ridge asked.

"Nelle says it's on Saturday." Sissy couldn't believe a father would forget his own daughter's birthday.

"Well, so it is." He paused. "Saturday's our busiest night. I don't think we can do it."

"Oh, it won't be any work," Nelle said. "We just thought we'd give Essie a cake with candles on it and everybody would sing 'Happy Birthday' to her. Please, Pa."

"Our cakes are for the customers. We can't spare one just for Essie's birthday."

"That's okay, we can make one," Sissy said, though she had no idea how to bake a cake.

Mr. Ridge stood up and jingled the coins in his pocket as he thought that over. "I suppose the diners might like that. They might give Essie extra tips," he said to himself. He nodded to Nelle. "All right, but you still have to waitress. I don't want this taking up time."

"Jack and I will do everything," Sissy said. "That's a good idea anyway. Then Essie won't be suspicious."

"So, how do we bake a cake?" Jack asked as the two left the Ridge house.

"It can't be too hard. Greenie has a cookbook. All we have to do is follow the directions." Sissy kicked a rock in the dirt road. "Maybe we better bake one tomorrow for practice. We can do it at my house."

"I'll bring the flour. How much do we need?"

"A handful," Sissy said, remembering how Greenie

reached into the flour bin when she made a cake.

"Your hand or mine?" Jack asked slyly.

"Maybe yours. It's bigger."

In the morning, Jack came to the Carlsons' house with a tin can full of flour. Sissy took down one of Greenie's cookbooks and studied it while Jack built up the fire in the cookstove.

"What are you doing?" Greenie asked, coming into the kitchen.

"We're making a cake for Essie Ridge's birthday. It's a surprise. We thought we'd make a practice one first so we're sure to get it right."

"I can help you when I get back from the store."

"Oh, that's all right. We can do it." Sissy had seen Greenie make cakes a hundred times. It looked easy enough. She got out Greenie's big yellow bowl. "I thought we could make devil's food cake. Everybody likes chocolate. Here's the recipe." She handed the *Church of Tenmile Cookbook* to Jack.

1 cup butter creamed with 1 cup sugar.

2 eggs.

½ cup chocolate grated in hot water.

⅔ cup sweet milk in which 1 teaspoon soda is dissolved.

2 cups flour.

1 teaspoon baking powder.

1 teaspoon vanilla.

Add whites of eggs last.

"It doesn't tell you how to do it," Jack said.

Sissy shrugged. "Oh, it's pretty simple. You just mix everything together." She frowned. "But I'm not sure what it means to cream the butter and sugar."

Jack shrugged. "I think it means you stir them together."

"I could have figured that out." Sissy dumped the butter and sugar into a bowl and stirred. The mixture was lumpy.

Jack broke the chocolate into chunks with a hammer, then added it to a cup of water so it melted. "Done," he said, looking proud of himself.

They mixed in the other ingredients and poured them into a pan. Then they put the pan into the oven.

"How long do we bake it? It doesn't say," said Jack.

"Until it's done," Sissy told him. "I guess we just wait."

"I know—let's go outside. I'll teach you how to play baseball. It's a new game. I brought a ball. All we need is a stick."

They went outside and found a stick of kindling Jack thought would work. Then he showed Sissy how to pitch the ball so he could hit it with the stick. The ball was soft, made from an old stocking, and it didn't go far. Still, the two had fun until Jack wrinkled his nose and asked, "What stinks?"

"Our cake!" Sissy cried.

The two ran inside to find smoke coming from the cookstove. Sissy wrapped a towel around her hand while Jack opened the oven door. They both stood back as smoke came pouring out. Sissy reached in and pulled out the pan. The cake was black, and, even worse, it was only an inch high.

Jack and Sissy looked at each other. "Now what?" they asked at the same time.

"Maybe the chickens will eat it," Jack said.

"I don't think they can sing 'Happy Birthday.' "

The two sat at the kitchen table looking glum. Greenie came into the kitchen. She had just returned from the store.

"It smells like you finished the cake," she said.

Sissy shrugged and pointed to the pan on top of the stove.

Greenie surveyed the mess. "Maybe you forgot to beat the egg whites."

"Well, that's not all," Jack told her. "It's not going to be much of a surprise for Essie."

"I think I know how to fix it," Greenie told them.

Sissy and Jack looked up at her hopefully.

"Why don't I give it a try?"

"Really?" the two said together.

"Of course," Greenie said. "It's a good thing I bought another bar of chocolate at the store."

"You knew," Sissy said.

"Knew what?" Greenie said. "All I know is that two young people are trying hard to make a happy birthday for a little girl."

On Saturday night, Sissy and Jack sneaked into the kitchen of Delmonico's with a big chocolate cake in Greenie's cake carrier. Nelle was washing dishes. When she peeked at the cake, she grinned.

"It's beautiful. Essie will be so excited. Did you make it?"

"Greenie helped," Sissy said. She set down the cake and took ten candles from her pocket. "When do you want to give it to her?"

"How about now?" Nelle said. "But we have to ask my father first."

Mr. Ridge came in from the dining room. When he saw the cake, his eyes lit up.

"Can we take it in now?" Nelle asked.

"Now's a good time. The restaurant's full."

Nelle peered through a crack in the door. "Essie's busy. Let's do it."

Sissy stuck the candles in the cake. Then Jack lit them. Nelle started to pick up the cake, but Mr. Ridge grabbed it away.

"I'll carry it," he said.

Sissy didn't say anything, but she thought that wasn't fair. After all, the birthday surprise had been Nelle's idea. Still, it was Mr. Ridge's restaurant, and Mr. Ridge was Essie's father. He could do what he wanted.

Jack pushed open the door, and Mr. Ridge stepped

through it. The restaurant was crowded and noisy. A few people looked up and stared, but most were too busy eating to notice the cake. Jack picked up a fork and banged it against a glass. The diners stopped talking and eating and turned to look at them. Essie, her back to the door, didn't pay attention.

Sissy started singing. "Happy birthday . . ."

Jack and Nelle chimed in, ". . . to you . . ."

The diners picked up the words. "Happy birthday to you. Happy birthday, dear . . ." They stopped, not knowing whose birthday it was.

Sissy, Jack, and Nelle raised their voices. "Dear Essie!"

Then everybody finished the song. "Happy birthday to you!"

When she heard her name, Essie spun around. Her eyes widened when she saw the cake. "Oh!" she said loudly. Then she began to cry. The diners cheered and clapped and yelled, "Happy birthday!"

Essie rushed over to Nelle and put her arms around her sister. "Oh, Nelle, I didn't think you'd remembered my birthday!"

"Of course, we did," Mr. Ridge said in a loud voice.

Then he turned to the room. "Birthday cake is our specialty tonight. Ten cents. And there's a bowl here for tips if anyone wants to contribute for my daughter's birthday."

People clapped again, but Sissy and Jack looked at each other in dismay. This wasn't what Essie's birthday was about. Greenie had made the cake. Mr. Ridge didn't have any right to sell it. And Sissy could tell from Nelle's face that she didn't want people putting money in a bowl for Essie.

Essie was so busy smiling and laughing, crying and hugging her sister that she hadn't heard her father. "Thank you, Nelle. It's the best birthday I ever had," she said through her tears.

The next morning, Sissy went up above the house to her grove of aspen trees.

A squirrel was high up on a tree limb. It ran down when it saw her. Sissy had brought a piece of the burnt cake she and Jack had made, and she set it on a stump for the squirrel. She sat down on a large rock near the little animal.

"Sometimes things don't work out exactly the way you

plan them," Sissy told it.

The squirrel didn't respond.

"We planned the birthday surprise for Essie, but Mr. Ridge took it over. He turned it into a way to make money."

The squirrel waved its tail.

"Mr. Ridge sold every slice of Greenie's cake. He must have made a dollar."

A bird chirped, and the squirrel looked up.

"But maybe it doesn't matter. Essie was happy, and that's what counts. I ought to remember that and forget about Mr. Ridge."

The squirrel *tsk-tsk*ed as if it were speaking.

"You sound an awful lot like Greenie," Sissy said.

6

Sɪssʏ ᴡᴀs ᴘɪᴄᴋɪɴɢ ᴜᴘ ᴅɪʀᴛʏ cloths in the surgery when she heard a knock on the door. A patient who had burned his hand had just left, and Sissy thought maybe he'd returned because he'd forgotten something.

"Would you see to it, Sis?" Doc asked. He was putting away instruments.

Sissy opened the door. It was early summer now, her favorite time of year. Wind had blown away the smelter smoke, and the sky was bright blue. The jack pines stood out dark green against the mountainsides. Sissy wondered what the Tenmile Range had looked like before the Yellowcat Mine was constructed. Before the shacks were built on Chicken Flats. Before the crooked roads and mine dumps had spoiled the hillsides.

She smelled the man before she saw him. He was stout and dressed in worn, ragged clothes. His hands and face were dirty. Tobacco juice stained his white beard.

"I'm not feeling hardy. Where's Doc?" he demanded. He moved so close to Sissy that she stepped back. He didn't take off his hat like most men did.

Sissy was tempted to hold her nose because the man smelled so bad. "He's inside," she said.

"Well, step aside, girl." The man pushed past Sissy and into Doc's office.

"I'll get the doctor," Sissy said, not asking the man to sit down. She went into the surgery and closed the door.

"That awful Tincup Charlie is here," she whispered. "If I'd known it was him, I wouldn't have opened the door. I don't think he's taken a bath or washed his clothes since the last time he was here. He also smells like he's drunk as a sow."

Sissy had seen Tincup Charlie Marion around Tenmile and knew he was a prospector who roamed the mountains with his burro in the summer, looking for gold. He spent all his money in the saloons. Sissy had seen him stumbling out of one, drunker than twenty dollars. Once she'd passed him sleeping in the street. He'd earned his nickname from the tin cup he used to beg for money.

Doc nodded. "What's wrong with him?"

"I didn't ask."

"Why is that?"

"Oh, Papa, I couldn't bear to stand next to him. He smells so awful."

Doc finished with his instruments, then went into his office. He frowned when he saw the man was still standing. "Have a seat, Charlie. How's the hunt for gold going?"

Charlie sat down in Doc's desk chair. "I found a gold streak in my claim. I reckon the ore'll assay out pretty good. All's I need is a grubstake, if you know somebody wishing to get rich."

Sissy knew this meant he was looking for someone who would stake him for grub and equipment in exchange for part interest in anything he discovered. She couldn't imagine anybody dumb enough to grubstake Tincup Charlie.

"I'll keep that in mind. Now, what seems to be the problem?"

The man put his feet up on Doc's desk. *I'm going to have to wash it after he leaves. Maybe the chair, too*, Sissy thought.

Charlie put his hand to his jaw and winced in pain. "I got a tooth that's gone bad, Doc. Hurts so's I can't sleep. I put tobacco on it, but it didn't do no good."

"No, I guess it wouldn't."

"So I figured you could pull it out."

Because Tenmile didn't have a dentist, Doc sometimes extracted abscessed teeth.

"Come on back into the surgery and let me take a look," Doc said. "Sissy, help me keep his mouth open."

Sissy held back. She had helped Doc extract teeth before, but the idea of standing next to this man who not only smelled awful but had breath bad enough to kill an iron statue of a dog sickened her.

Doc gave her a long look, then examined the man's mouth by himself. Charlie had only a few teeth left, so it was obvious which one had gone bad. "I'll take it out," Doc said. "Sissy, I need your help."

She shook her head and mouthed, "I can't."

Doc ignored her and said, "Get out the instruments."

"She's naught but a girl. She don't know nothing," Charlie said.

Sissy bristled.

"She's my helper," Doc told him. "She will assist me."

The man studied Sissy for a moment. "If you say so, Doc."

Sissy washed the implement that Doc used to extract teeth.

"Hold his head still," Doc ordered.

Sissy wished she could hold her nose. Instead, she turned her face away as she put her hands on his dirty head.

After Doc removed the tooth, he handed it to Sissy. She threw it into the wastebasket.

"Hey, I want that tooth. Give it to me, girl!" Charlie bellowed. "I can wear it on my watch chain. When I get a chain. And a watch."

Sissy fished out the tooth and handed it to him. "Here," she said. The tooth was black and broken. Sissy was disgusted. Why would anyone want to keep it?

Charlie held out his dirty hand and grinned at the tooth. "Say, Doc, you don't have anything for the pain, do you? What do you say I try a little whiskey?"

Sissy assumed her father would tell him to go to the saloon, but instead Doc said, "Sis, would you ask Mrs. Greenway for a glass of whiskey?"

Sissy was shocked. Doc never gave clients hard liquor. "Are you sure?"

Doc gave her a stern look. "Do I have to tell you twice?"

"No, sir." Sissy was stung by her father's harsh words. She went into the kitchen and returned with the liquor.

Charlie gulped it down and held out the glass. "I sure could use another."

"I think one will do. The whiskey should help heal the cavity where the tooth was."

Now Sissy understood. Doc wanted to sterilize the man's mouth.

Charlie stood up slowly. He glanced around the room as if looking for a place to sleep. *Please don't let him stay in the spare bedroom, Papa,* Sissy thought.

The man seemed to accept that he wouldn't get any more liquor and started for the door. "Maybe I'll get me another drink at the saloon. Somebody there's liable to feel sorry for a sick man."

He started for the door, and Sissy said, "Mr. Marion,

Doc charges a dollar to take out a tooth."

"I'll have to pay you later," he said. He opened the door and started ambling down the street.

Sissy left the door open to air out the office and surgery. "He didn't even pay," she said.

"My work is more important than getting paid," Doc told her. "I think you know that."

"It's not right! He's a drunk, and he's so lazy he won't get out of bed for less than a dollar. Next time he comes here, I'll slam the door in his face."

"You'll do no such thing." Doc studied Sissy, then said quietly, "I'm disappointed in you, Sis. He is a patient. He needed our help. You should have treated him with respect no matter how foul he smelled or how he looked. Doctors take an oath to help everyone. It doesn't matter who they are or whether they can pay. You should be ashamed of yourself."

Sissy's face turned red. She started for the surgery, but Doc said, "I'll clean up. You run along."

She bowed her head. She knew he was right.

Sissy left the house and walked up the mountain to her grove. She sat down on the fallen tree trunk and stared up at the clouds. There was a breeze in the aspen that made the leaves jiggle, and soon she heard a squirrel begin to chatter.

"Oh, shut up. Why should I have to be nice to Tincup Charlie? He stinks, and he's a miser," Sissy said.

But maybe I should have been kinder, she thought. *Greenie's always saying we should be nice to everybody, especially those who have less than we do.*

The squirrel ran down the tree and perched on a rock. "But Papa didn't have to get mad at me," she told the squirrel. "I'm trying the best I can."

Sissy wished she'd brought something to feed the squirrel. The little creature was helping her think. *Papa's right. I guess I need to do better.*

She turned to the squirrel. "All right, you win. You're almost as good as Jack to talk things over with." Sissy leaned against a rock and watched the squirrel run off. "Thanks," she called.

7

A WEEK LATER, SISSY AWOKE to rain—cold mountain rain. But by noon, the sun had come out and warmed things. Greenie said, "It's a perfect day to hunt mushrooms. Let's invite Nelle and Martha to come along with us."

Sissy ran down to Chicken Flats to ask Nelle if she wanted to go.

"We're going to collect mushrooms," Sissy explained when Mr. Ridge opened the door. "Can Nelle come along?"

He thought that over. "We could use some mushrooms at the restaurant. Be sure you get a full pail, and don't be long, Nelle. There's work to do."

The two rushed over to Martha's house. "Martha, we're going mushrooming. Come with us," Sissy said.

Mrs. Popov, Martha's mother, smiled. "You get some nice fat ones. I'll fry them for supper." She handed Martha a basket.

The three hurried back to Sissy's house. Then Greenie and the girls, baskets over their arms, started up the mountain. They walked a mile, high into the Tenmile Range. They climbed until they couldn't see the town anymore. The sounds of the mine and the mill were faint. They could hear birdsong now. The air was clear of the smoke that hung over the town. Fringes of winter snow still crusted the mountain peaks—snow that was old and dirty and would stay until next winter's storms covered it up. The hot sun had melted everything along the trail except for the snow in the deep shadows of the pine trees. Sissy knew she would be sunburned by the time they returned home. She heard the buzz of insects. Dust devils swirled. Startled by their approach, a blue jay flew up. A mosquito landed on Sissy's arm, and she smashed it. She wished she had remembered to rub her arms with leaves from a tansy bush to keep the mosquitoes away.

The mountains were covered with tall, sparse pine trees and aspen with their quaking green leaves. Underneath them were wildflowers. "Look! There are prairie fire and butter-and-eggs," Martha said.

"My favorite flowers are summer's-half-over," Nelle told them. The tall stalks of bright pink flowers bloomed midway between the last snow of spring and the first snow of fall. Summers in the high country were short, but they were beautiful. Sissy was glad for a chance to be away from the town.

"This looks like a good place to stop," said Greenie. She set down the picnic basket and opened it up. The four of them sat on a log, their backs to the sun, as they ate their sandwiches. There were cookies, too. Sissy fed part of hers to a gray squirrel that chattered from a nearby stump.

She leaned against a pine tree, feeling the rough bark on her back. "How come the mountains can't be like this all the time?" she asked. "In another couple of months, the mountains are going to be covered with ice and snow. Winter lasts so long up here." She remembered Greenie saying it seemed like Tenmile had two seasons: this winter and last winter.

"God gives us the summers to make up for the winters," Greenie said now. She shooed away a golden bee. "Let's get to mushrooming." She picked up her basket, and the four began searching along the deer trails and under the dark green pines.

It was early in the season for mushrooms, but the morning rain had caused some of them to pop up. Sissy knew what to look for. She hunted for umbrella-shaped mushrooms with gills under a brown cap and for whitish ones that looked as if they'd been dipped in milk gone bad.

"Don't pick the red ones," she told Nelle and Martha. "They're the prettiest ones. They look like fairy toadstools in a children's book, but they'll make you very sick." She had been with Doc when he'd treated a child who'd eaten one.

Sissy saw a clump of mushrooms near a rotting log. She turned one over to make sure there were no worm holes. She plucked several and added them to Nelle's basket. Then she spotted a feather the color of grapes and put it into her own basket. Greenie was the fastest and had already picked dozens of mushrooms.

"I'll fry them in butter tonight," Greenie said. "We'll dry the rest in the cookstove and store them in a big glass jar.

That way we can use them in soups and stews in the winter."

It was fun hunting for mushrooms. Sissy found them beside rocks and old logs. She wandered through the pines, her eyes on the ground. Suddenly, she smelled smoke and looked up. In front of her was a crude log cabin in a stand of timber. Sissy thought it looked like a prospector's cabin. She knew that prospectors spent the summers in the mountains looking for gold and silver, and they lived in these rough dwellings. This one was tidier than most, she thought, with the yard raked clean of pine needles. A burlap bag hung as a curtain in the one window. A burro stood beside the cabin. A little girl was in front of it, her black hair in a braid down her back.

"Hi," Sissy said.

The girl didn't reply. Instead, she darted inside. A moment later, a woman came out. She waved.

Sissy smiled and walked toward the cabin. "Hi," she said again.

"Hello, yourself," the woman replied. "We don't get us many visitors up here. Come inside and sit you down."

Greenie and the other girls had just come up. Greenie said, "Why, I believe you're Mrs. Washington. I saw you at the store down in Tenmile."

"I guess I am. You call me Willow Louise."

The woman pronounced her name "Willer." Sissy didn't understand it until Greenie repeated, "Yes, Willow Louise."

"My name's Sissy, and these are my friends Nelle and Martha," Sissy said.

Willow Louise leaned against the doorframe. She smelled of woodsmoke. "We're from down south. My husband come here to find gold. He ain't found none yet, but he's looking. I expect he'll find a gold mine before long. This here is Sarah. She's on to eight years old."

The little girl put one bare foot on top of the other and stared at the ground. Every now and then, she glanced up at the older girls, then looked quickly away.

"Oh, Sarah, that's my favorite name," Martha said.

"Is that your doll?" Sissy asked. She nodded at a rag doll in Sarah's hand. "Is her name Sarah, too?"

"No. That's silly," the girl said. She paused, then said in a low voice, "Betsy."

" 'Sweet Betsy from Pike,' " Willow Louise said. "You girls know that song, do you?"

The three girls sang the first lines together:

"Oh, do you remember sweet Betsy from Pike, who crossed the wide prairies with her brother Ike . . ."

Sarah lisped softly, "With two yoke of cattle and one yellow dog . . ." She stopped, embarrassed.

"A tall Shanghai rooster and one spotted hog," Sissy finished.

The girl smiled shyly, and Martha asked, "May I hold Betsy?"

Sarah thought it over, then handed the doll to Martha. In return, Sissy gave Sarah the feather she had found. Sarah put it into her braid. A moment later, she was chattering with the girls as if they were old friends.

"You must enjoy it, living up here in God's country," Greenie said to Willow Louise.

"I reckon I do, but I have a hard time with my cooking. My beans just never get done."

"That's because of the altitude. Water boils at a lower temperature in the mountains."

"Well, I don't understand that." Willow Louise looked confused.

"Just start cooking your Sunday dinner beans on Friday night and you'll be fine," Greenie said.

Willow Louise laughed. "I understand that all right."

Greenie offered Willow Louise some mushrooms, but the woman shook her head. "I have a plenty of them. I just go outside my door and pick as many as I want. I don't suppose they'll grow here in winter, though."

"You're staying up here for the winter?" Sissy gasped.

"We got it real nice here."

"But you can't stay through the winter. Winters in the Tenmile Range are harsh," Sissy said, remembering how blizzards swept through the mountains, bringing temperatures below zero and leaving drifts of snow as high as a house.

"I don't know why not."

"You'll freeze," Nelle said.

"Where are you from?" Greenie asked.

"Down near White Pigeon."

"In the South, you said."

"Yes, ma'am."

Greenie nodded. "I figured as much. The Tenmile isn't much like the South."

Before Greenie could explain further about Tenmile winters, Nelle looked up and saw the sun was midway down the sky. "I got to get home. Pa will . . . Pa will be upset if I'm late."

"Time we went, too," Greenie said. She bent over and picked up her basket. "We sure appreciate the visit," she told Willow Louise.

"You come back anytime. Maybe my mister will be here."

Nelle handed the doll back to Sarah. "Can I visit Betsy again?"

"She likes you to visit," the little girl said shyly.

Greenie and the three girls started back down the trail. It would take an hour to reach Tenmile, and Nelle was eager to get home.

"They're not really going to stay up there all winter, are they?" Sissy asked.

"Not after the first snow." Greenie laughed.

When they reached Tenmile, Nelle thanked Greenie for letting her tag along. Greenie looked into Nelle's basket and saw it was only half full.

"You take some of my findings," Greenie said, pouring half of her mushrooms into Nelle's basket. "Sissy and Martha have enough. There'll be plenty more to pick this summer. Going mushrooming will be a good excuse for me to call on

Willow Louise again."

Nelle and Martha hurried on toward Chicken Flats.

"How come you gave Nelle your mushrooms? I thought you were going to dry the ones you don't fry tonight," Sissy asked.

Greenie smiled. "Oh, I guess I don't feel like standing over the cookstove in this heat, drying mushrooms."

"That's not it at all, is it?" Sissy asked, wondering how Greenie knew that Mr. Ridge expected Nelle to bring home a full pail. "I'm on to you, Greenie."

8

Sissy knew that most of the boys in Chicken Flats worked to earn money for their families. A boy she knew milked his family's cow and sold the milk. Some of the boys at school peddled candy, gum, and magazines to people waiting at the depot or carried passengers' luggage to the trains. Some worked in stores or as ushers at the theaters. Sissy's friends looked for iron and scrap lumber they could sell. They also collected sawdust from the sawmill and sold it to saloons to sprinkle on their floors. The sawdust absorbed spilled drinks as well as the snow and water customers tracked in.

Older, stronger boys got jobs on grocery wagons. They

held the horses and fought anybody who tried to steal the goods while the drivers made deliveries. During election years, candidates hired Jack and his brother Peter to pass out cards and carry banners. The boys also supplied wood for bonfires at rallies. "Backyard fences make the best fires," Jack told Sissy with a sly grin.

Sissy's friends from Chicken Flats collected beer bottles and sold them three for a nickel to breweries. Heavy woven gunny sacks brought in two cents each. "I can't put out one for a doormat without some kid snatching it away," Greenie complained.

Sissy was aware that life was not easy for the children of Chicken Flats. She was especially sorry for the boys who had to quit school and work in the mines.

One afternoon in early summer, Jack and Sissy were walking to Jack's house, each of them carrying a bucket. They'd been picking up coal.

Jack said, "I can't go with you to collect coal anymore."

"How come?" Her bucket of coal was heavy, and Sissy

switched it from one hand to the other. She looked up at Jack and grinned. "Did you get a job selling newspapers?"

Selling newspapers before and after school would be a fine job for Jack. He'd make good money, and not just from the price of the papers. Jack had told her the gamblers and mining men who bought newspapers generally tipped, sometimes as much as a dollar. Jack had often talked about getting a part-time job as a newsboy to help his family.

Jack shook his head. "I have to go underground." There was a catch in his throat.

"Underground! What do you mean?"

Jack repeated, "I'm going underground. I have to. I have a job."

"For the rest of the summer?" Sissy held her breath.

Jack shook his head. "It's permanent."

"You mean a real job? You're going to work in the mine for good?" Sissy gasped.

Jack nodded. "I won't be able to go back to school."

"But you have to. You're going to graduate from high school and then go on to college."

"Maybe Peter can go instead one day."

"Jack!" Sissy stopped walking and set down her bucket.

She put her hands on her hips. "You're not quitting school! You can't! You have plans!"

"Not anymore. I can't help it, Sissy. I don't have a choice. We need the money." He placed his bucket beside Sissy's and turned away, but not before Sissy saw that he was crying.

"What happened?" she asked softly.

"My father." Jack put his foot on a rock to steady himself and turned back to Sissy. "Pa gambles. It's never been much of a problem before. Last week, he had a good hand, the best. He thought he could win enough to help send me to college. But he's a poor gambler. Somebody else had an even better hand. Pa lost a whole lot of money. He didn't have it, so he gave an IOU."

"And *you* have to work to help pay it off?"

Jack nodded. "I've already got a job at the Yellowcat."

"That's awful! Why would he think he could make money gambling? He's spoiled everything!" Sissy said. She thought that over. "But you can go back to school after the debt's paid, right?"

"When did you ever hear of anybody leaving underground, except to die?" Jack asked bitterly. "Mining's going to be my life forever."

"You can't quit, Jack. I'll bring your lessons to you."

Jack thought about that. "I don't think so, Sissy."

"You can do it. Promise me you'll try." Sissy handed her coal bucket to Jack to add to what he'd collected.

"How can I? Working underground is hard. I'll be too tired to study. Besides, no teacher would agree to that. He didn't mean to, but Pa ruined my life." Jack shook his head. "And he was the one who made me want to go to college. He used to brag to his friends that I'd get out of Tenmile. Now I'm stuck here forever."

Sissy thought that was the saddest thing she'd ever heard.

That night at supper, Sissy told Doc and Greenie that Jack was going to quit school to work at the Yellowcat.

"What?" Greenie exclaimed. "I thought that boy was planning for something better. He was going to be an example to the other boys in Chicken Flats."

"That's what he is now—an example showing you can't get away," Sissy said bitterly. She explained what had happened. "I told him he could go back to school when the debt was paid."

Doc shook his head. "Once they go underground, they never come back. I hate to say it, but he's stuck for life."

"Trapped, you mean," Greenie said. "Trapped by a man foolish enough to ruin his son's future by gambling."

Doc nodded. "It's a shame anybody ever encouraged Jack to go to college. That makes it all the harder for him now that things haven't turned out right."

Sissy just stared at her father.

After the dishes were done, Sissy put on her sweater and hiked up to her grove of aspen trees to think. Was what Doc had said about college meant for her, too? Would Doc keep her from going away to school? Did he expect her to spend the rest of her life in Tenmile?

The squirrel came into the clearing and chattered. Sissy tossed a rock at it. "Get out of here, you dumb thing. Don't you dare tell me everything will be all right."

The squirrel ran off, and Sissy lay down in the long grass, thinking. Jack was a boy. If he couldn't go to college, how could she? Girls didn't have any control over their lives. She couldn't just run off and get a job someplace. Even if she did, what kind of job would it be? She'd have to be a waitress like Nelle or a housekeeper like Greenie. Those jobs didn't pay enough to live on, let alone save enough for college.

Sissy plucked a long blade of grass and chewed on the end. Then she tossed it aside. Were her chances any better than Jack's? Maybe they were both stuck in Tenmile.

9

AFTER JACK STARTED WORKING IN the Yellowcat, Sissy stopped at his house on his day off to see him. She'd brought a book for the two of them to read together, but Jack said he was too tired to read.

A week later, she waited by the road to the mine when she knew Jack was coming off shift. His face was covered with grime, and he carried a dinner bucket just like the other miners. He looked away as she approached and only grunted hello, as if he was embarrassed that Sissy recognized him.

At school, she asked Peter how Jack was doing.

"I don't know why he quit school. I guess he didn't like

it anymore," Peter said.

Sissy wasn't surprised Peter didn't know. Apparently, Jack hadn't told him because he didn't want to shame his father. "Does he read his schoolbooks?"

"Naw. He gave them to me. Jack's a miner now. I'm the one going to college." Peter stuck out his chest.

Sissy wanted to tell him not to count on it. But why spoil Peter's dream?

One afternoon a couple of weeks after Jack started working at the Yellowcat, Sissy came home from Martha's to see a group of miners milling around outside their house.

"What happened? Was somebody hurt in the mine? Does Doc need me?" she asked.

She hurried into the surgery. Peter was standing outside the closed door.

"Pete! What are you doing here? What's wrong?" Sissy held her breath. There was only one reason Peter would be there: Either Jack or Mr. Burke had been hurt. *Please not Jack*, she prayed.

"It's Jack! I was on my way home when I saw them bringing him here. Sissy, they said Jack's hurt bad."

Sissy gripped Peter's hand. "What happened?"

Peter started to reply, but Doc called through the closed door, "Sissy, is that you? Will you come in here, please?"

Two men were standing near the operating table, and they moved back as Sissy approached. They held their caps in their hands and wouldn't look Sissy in the eye. She gasped when she saw Jack lying on his back, his eyes closed. He wasn't moving. One of his legs was bent at an awkward angle.

Sissy bit her lip to hold back the tears. "What happened, Papa? Is he dead?"

Doc shook his head, then looked at one of the miners, who said, "We were setting off dynamite charges. Near as we can figure, Jack went into the blasting area too soon, and the rock ceiling fell on him."

"He was green. He'd been underground only a couple of weeks. He didn't know how long to wait," the second miner said, rubbing a hand over his face.

"Let me take a look at him," Doc said. "It's pretty crowded in here. Would you boys mind waiting outside?"

The two men went out and joined the other miners.

It was getting dark, and Greenie brought in kerosene lamps and set them around the room. She took Sissy's arm and said, "You don't need to see this. Help me make coffee in the kitchen."

Sissy pulled away. "He's my friend, Greenie. I'm staying here. Doc needs me."

She turned to Doc, who was examining Jack. Peter had sneaked into the room and was staring at his brother. When Doc saw him, he said, "You'd better get your folks, son."

Peter dashed out the door. By the time he returned from Chicken Flats with his parents, Doc had finished examining Jack and had begun setting his leg.

Jack's parents hurried into the surgery. Mrs. Burke held baby Nancy. Mr. Burke shook his head. "I heard there was an accident. I didn't know it was Jack until Peter came for us," he stammered. "How bad is it, Doc?"

Doc escorted the Burkes into his office, and Sissy followed. "It's not good, Mr. Burke."

"I never should have let him go underground," Mr. Burke said. "It's my fault. It's my own damn fault." He slammed his hand against the doorjamb.

"Is he going to be all right?" Mrs. Burke whispered. She

clutched Nancy so hard that the baby began to cry.

Doc took a deep breath. "I don't know. He has some broken bones in his leg. I hope I can save it. But the bigger worry is his head. He got hit pretty hard when the rocks fell."

"Oh!" Mrs. Burke cried. She sagged against the table. Her husband grabbed her to keep her from falling. The two held on to each other.

"You're sure it's that bad, Doc?" Mr. Burke asked. His wife reached up and wiped tears from his face.

"No, I'm not sure of anything, but from the looks of it, he could have a concussion."

"He'll get well," Peter said. "He's Jack. He can do anything. Sissy knows that."

"If anybody can recover from this, it's Jack, all right," Doc said. "But I don't want to give you false hope."

Mrs. Burke sobbed, "Jackie! Jackie!" Mr. Burke coughed and cleared his throat. Then he went to the open front door, where the men were waiting. A group of Jack's and Sissy's friends was with them. Nelle and Martha sat on the porch steps.

Sissy wondered how they knew Jack was hurt, but bad news traveled fast in Tenmile.

"There's nothing you folks can do for Jack. You go on home, now. But you might say a little prayer for him," Mr. Burke said.

Peter left with the others. Little Joe was at home by himself and needed watching over. Mr. and Mrs. Burke stayed, sitting by Jack's side all night. So did Sissy.

Early in the morning, Sissy heard a knock on the office door. Greenie was fixing breakfast, and Doc was checking on Jack. The Burkes had gone home. Sissy hoped it wasn't someone asking about her friend. She didn't know what to say, since Jack's condition hadn't changed. She wished she could leave the house. She wanted to hike up to her special place, where she could cry her eyes out without anyone seeing her.

Sissy opened the door. A tall gray-haired man in a fine wool suit stood there. A gold watch chain stretched across his stomach. "Is Doctor Carlson in? I'm Mr. Gilpin. I've come to inquire about Jack Burke," he said.

Sissy knew Mr. Gilpin was the owner of the Yellowcat Mine. She had seen him in Tenmile, but she'd never met him. For a moment, she was tongue-tied. Then she said, "Doc's in the surgery with Jack. He'll have to tell you how he is."

Doc heard the two talking and came into the office. "Hello, Mr. Gilpin."

"Hello, Doc. Your nurse and I were just discussing Jack."

"Sissy's my daughter. She and Jack are friends." He turned to Sissy. "You can go help Mrs. Greenway. Try to get Jack to eat something when he wakes up."

"Yes, sir."

Sissy started for the kitchen, but Mr. Gilpin held up his hand. "May I ask you to come to my office every now and then, Sissy, to report on how Jack's getting along?"

Sissy was taken aback. From all the miners' grumbling about the working conditions at the Yellowcat, she'd assumed Mr. Gilpin would be a stuffy, unpleasant man, but he seemed to care about Jack. She wondered how the rich Yellowcat owner even knew about a poor Chicken Flats boy who worked for him.

10

A WEEK AFTER JACK RETURNED home, he hadn't improved. Sissy had accompanied Greenie twice when she took supper to the Burkes, but both times Jack had been asleep, so she wasn't able to talk to him.

Greenie went to visit a friend who lived over in Middle Swan. She left Sissy in charge of meals, but Sissy wasn't any better at cooking than she was at baking cakes. She studied Greenie's cookbooks, but still she burned the meat and overcooked the vegetables. The bread she baked turned out as flat as a cracker. After three nights of Sissy's cooking, Doc said he would take her to a restaurant for supper. He asked her to choose a place.

Tenmile had a dozen restaurants. Doc and Sissy had eaten in almost all of them. "Do you want to go to the hotel?" Doc asked. The hotel dining room was the most elegant eating place in town. The room had carved wood paneling and satin drapes. The menu was in French, and the waiters wore formal clothes. Sissy had seen Mr. Gilpin eating there. She loved the food, but the atmosphere made her uncomfortable. She was afraid she'd spill something or talk too loudly and the waiters would frown.

Sissy shook her head.

Sometimes the two of them ate at the chop suey café. They'd dined at the Mexican place and the two Italian restaurants and the one run by a Finn. They'd even tried the hash house that catered to the miners.

Wherever they went, people greeted Sissy's father. "Hey, Doc, my arm's just fine," one said. Another woman held up a baby Doc had delivered and said he was already two years old. And a man told Doc the abscess on his toe was gone. "Here, I'll show you," he said as he started taking off his boot.

"I'll take your word for it," Doc had said.

Sissy was proud of her father. People loved him. She wondered what would happen to the folks in Tenmile if her father left. She'd asked him once why he hadn't moved to Denver, where there were beautiful houses and grass and leafy trees. "Because people in Tenmile need me," he'd replied.

That night, she considered the different restaurants, then picked Delmonico's. Doc wasn't surprised. It had always been Sissy's favorite eatery since Nelle's family owned it and Nelle worked there. Delmonico's was a friendly, informal place. The tables were covered with red-and-white checked tablecloths. In the summer, each table had a vase of wildflowers. Sometimes Sissy helped Nelle pick them.

Sissy chose the table closest to the front window. She liked to watch people walking up and down the street. There were miners on their way to work or coming off shift carrying their dinner buckets. Men in bowler hats and business suits passed by wearing heavy gold watch chains across their stomachs, just like Mr. Gilpin. She saw gamblers in string ties and brocade vests sharing the sidewalk with grizzled old prospectors, called sourdoughs. They reminded Sissy of Tincup Charlie. Once she spotted the famous actor Eddie Foy strolling by on his way to the theater.

Delmonico's menu was written on a blackboard with "All Meals Fifty Cents." Sissy studied it for a long time, unable to make up her mind. She considered roast turkey, or maybe the mountain trout. Perhaps pot roast with brown gravy? She finally decided on Virginia ham with raisin sauce, the restaurant's specialty. Doc ordered fried oysters. He always chose fried oysters. "They come all the way from the ocean. They're packed in sawdust and shipped west in big barrels on the train," he'd once explained.

Nelle came to take their order, smiling when she saw Sissy. Both girls had been busy and hadn't spoken much since the night of Jack's injury. "How's Jack?" Nelle asked.

Sissy glanced at her father, who nodded at her to answer. "About the same. It's really too early to tell."

"I hope he'll be all right."

"Me, too."

Mr. Ridge came over to their table, too. He shook hands with Doc and slapped him on the back. He turned to a man at the next table and said, "Dr. Carlson is the finest doctor on the Tenmile." Sissy thought that was funny. Papa was the only doctor on the Tenmile Range.

"And you, Miss Sissy—prettier than ever. Sugar and

spice and everything nice. Your father's going to have to keep a stick behind the door to keep the boys away. Time for you to find a husband."

Sissy knew he was teasing her since she was only thirteen.

"You girls have been in school too long," Mr. Ridge added.

"Hi, Mr. Ridge," Sissy said.

Doc nodded at him. He didn't comment.

After Mr. Ridge left, Sissy asked, "I don't understand what he meant by that remark. Do you think he'll take Nelle out of school before she graduates to work here full-time?"

"I wouldn't be surprised. Seems like he doesn't put too much stock in schooling," Doc said.

"Nelle's a good student. She ought to finish high school."

"I don't imagine she'll have much say in it. Mr. Ridge rules that family."

"Don't you like him?"

Doc didn't reply. Sissy thought that was odd. Doc liked almost everybody. Maybe he just didn't care for Mr. Ridge's jokes.

Doc changed the subject. "Have you been keeping Mr. Gilpin up to date about Jack?"

"I've been to the Yellowcat twice. I think Mr. Gilpin's secretary likes me—now anyway. The first time I went there, I told him I wanted to see Mr. Gilpin about something personal. I guess he mistook me for a Chicken Flats wife whose husband had been fired for drinking underground. He told me Mr. Gilpin wasn't going to give my husband his job back and to go away and not bother him." Sissy laughed. "But Mr. Gilpin heard me and said I was welcome anytime. So now the secretary lets me in."

Sissy was going to say more, but just then, Nelle brought their dinners. She looked tired and rushed. Sissy asked if she was anxious for classes to start in the fall—then she wouldn't have to spend every day in the restaurant. Nelle didn't answer, and Sissy thought Doc might be right. Maybe Nelle's father wasn't going to let her return to school.

"We're awful busy. I have to get back to the kitchen," Nelle said.

Sissy glanced around the room. The restaurant was indeed crowded. Nelle and Essie were the only waitresses. As Sissy watched, across the room Essie lost her grip on a heavy tray, and a load of plates and cups and glasses crashed to the floor. Everyone turned to stare. Essie's face went red with embarrassment. She also looked frightened. She backed up against a table and looked down at the floor. Mr. Ridge went over to her and grinned.

Then he said in a loud voice, "We call her butterfingers."

People laughed, but Essie didn't. Nelle hurried to her sister and whispered something. Then she helped Essie pick up the pieces of broken china and glass. Essie scurried into the kitchen with them. When Sissy turned back to her supper, she saw that Doc was watching her.

"Poor Essie," she said.

Doc nodded and started eating. After a time, he said. "If Essie cut her hand, how would you treat it?"

This was a game they played. Doc said that if she was going to help him with his patients, she ought to know a thing or two about medicine. In fact, Sissy thought she knew more than just a thing or two. Often, when she was stuck in the office with nothing to do, she read through his medical books.

Sissy cut a piece of her ham and ate it. "Clean the cut with soap and water first," she said. "Then apply alcohol to keep it from getting infected." She stopped eating and asked, "Is that right?"

"Good," Doc said. He swallowed an oyster. "What about gout?"

Sissy grinned. She knew what gout was since Doc had just treated someone for it and she had watched. It was an inflammation of the joints.

"Hot vinegar and table salt rubbed on with a piece of flannel." She sopped up raisin sauce with a piece of ham, then chewed it. "And tell the patient to stop drinking."

Doc smiled at that. "Rattlesnake bite?"

Sissy thought that over. "Suck the poison from the wound, then apply spirits of ammonia."

"Mountain fever?" Since that was a common ailment in the high mountains, Sissy had helped Doc treat several patients who had it.

"Um . . ." Sissy took her time. "I think comfrey. Then put the patient under blankets to sweat it out." She finished her potatoes while she waited to see if she was correct.

Doc swallowed his last oyster. "Yes, and what else?"

"Baking soda baths . . . and onion soup!"

"Onion soup? We don't have it," Nelle said.

Sissy and Doc were concentrating on the game and hadn't seen Nelle approach. "Oh, we don't want it," Sissy said. "We're playing a game. Papa's quizzing me on how to treat patients who have all kinds of things. He asked me what I'd do if Essie cut her hand on a piece of broken china." Sissy paused. "How is she?"

Nelle didn't exactly answer. "She didn't cut herself."

Doc ran a piece of bread across his plate to sop up the oyster sauce. "Is your sister all right?"

"Yes, sir." Nelle glanced at the kitchen door. Essie hadn't emerged since she'd dropped the tray.

"If she hurt herself, you bring her to me in the morning," Doc said. He reached for another piece of bread.

Nelle nodded. "I came to ask about dessert. We have only one piece of coconut cake left. I know it's your favorite, Sissy. Do you want me to save it for you?"

"You bet," Sissy said.

Nelle turned to Doc. He said, "I'll have apple pie."

"Sissy—" Nelle started to say, but at that moment, Mr. Ridge came up beside his daughter.

"Are you dawdling? We have other customers." He turned to Doc. "I hope your daughter isn't as distracted as my two." He didn't smile or shake his head. Sissy wondered if he was serious.

"No, sir," Nelle said. "I was taking their dessert order."

"Coconut cake, I'll wager," he said, grinning at Sissy.
She nodded.

"And did you get Doc Carlson's order?" Mr. Ridge asked
Nelle.

She started to reply, but Doc interrupted. "I changed my
mind. I'll just have coffee."

Mr. Ridge and Nelle left, and Doc stared at the kitchen
door.

"Nelle said Essie was all right, but do you want me to go
see if she's really okay?" Sissy asked.

"No. We can't treat people who don't want to be helped."

Sissy didn't understand. "What do you mean?"

Doc didn't answer, and soon Nelle brought his coffee
and Sissy's cake. Nelle set the items down on the table. Sissy,
trying to figure out what Doc meant, only picked at the
cake. She smashed some of it with her fork to make it look
like she'd eaten more.

Doc paid for their dinners and left a twenty-five-cent
tip. Sissy knew the money wouldn't go to Nelle. She'd put
it in a jar in the back for her father. She suspected Essie's
birthday tips had gone there, too. Doc must have known

about the tips, because he slipped a dime into Nelle's pocket and said, "You treat your sister." Then he told Nelle again, "Bring Essie to see me if she's hurt."

11

THE NEXT MORNING, SISSY ANSWERED a knock on the office door. Nelle and Essie stood there. Despite the summer heat, the younger girl was wearing a long-sleeved dress and a bonnet.

Nelle looked surprised to see Sissy. "Oh, I didn't know you'd be here."

"I'm helping Papa today."

"I'll come back," Nelle said. She turned away.

Essie looked up. Although the bonnet covered part of the girl's face, Sissy could see bruises. There was also a cut on her lip.

"Oh!" Sissy exclaimed. "What happened?"

"She fell," Nelle said.

"I thought she cut her hand last night."

Nelle shook her head. "I don't know why we came here. Essie's okay." She started to leave.

"Nelle!" Sissy said sharply. "Doc doesn't talk about his patients. I don't, either. Anything that happens here, we keep to ourselves. Let Doc take a look at her."

"Please, Nelle, it hurts," Essie whispered.

Nelle paused, seeming to consider what Sissy had said, then nodded.

Once the sisters were settled in the office, Sissy went to fetch her father. "Nelle and Essie are here, and Essie's hurt," she said.

"I was afraid of that. How bad is it?"

"I just saw part of her face. I don't understand. She didn't fall last night at the restaurant."

Doc nodded. Then he took her hands. "Sissy, you're going to learn some hard things today. I think you are grown-up enough to understand." He paused. "I want to remind you that you are not to gossip."

"I already told Nelle I wouldn't."

"Come along. We'll see how bad it is," Doc said.

Essie was seated on a chair in the office. Doc knelt down beside her and removed her bonnet. Sissy gasped when she saw that the girl had a black eye.

"Show him your wrist," Nelle told her sister. Essie held it up.

Doc examined it. He said, "Fortunately, it's not broken." He stood and looked at Nelle. "What happened?"

"Pa said she'd broken five dollars' worth of dishes and he was going to teach her a lesson so she'd never do it again. I tried to protect her. I said it wasn't Essie's fault."

Despite knowing she should keep quiet, Sissy whispered. "Your father did that to Essie?"

Nelle looked away, embarrassed. Doc gave Sissy a stern look.

"I tried to stop him." Nelle began to cry. "Doc Carlson, it's gotten so much worse since Ma died. I don't care about me. I can take it. But Essie, she's a little girl."

After the two left, Sissy said to her father, "I don't understand.

Why did Mr. Ridge hit Essie?"

Doc sat down at his desk and looked out the window. The air was warm, and the flowers Greenie had planted were blooming. Bees buzzed around the window.

"I don't know, Sis. Some men—some people—are like that. They get angry, and they can't stop themselves. I'm sorry you had to learn about this."

"But he's always so nice. It's not like he's some old tramp."

"Sometimes people are nice to outsiders but act like monsters in their own homes. You can't judge from appearances. People think Mr. Ridge is a kind man because he is so friendly at the restaurant. But as you now know, he is a violent father."

"I've seen bruises on Nelle, too. Last year she had a broken arm." Sissy thought about that. "You fixed it, didn't you? Did you know what was going on?"

Doc didn't answer her question. Instead, he said, "She might have been embarrassed about what happened. She came to see me when she knew you were at school so you wouldn't find out."

Sissy wished she'd known. She wished she understood why it had happened, too.

"Why didn't you talk to Mr. Ridge?"

"I did. I thought it had stopped, but I was wrong."

Later that day, as Sissy sat on the log in the aspen grove, she thought about Nelle and Essie—and about Jack, too. Although she visited him as often as she could, she hadn't seen much change in his condition. She grieved for her friends. Life was so hard on the Tenmile. Was it this hard in other places? Her friends were suffering, and she didn't know why. It wasn't fair. She looked around for the squirrel, wondering if he'd disagree with her, but he wasn't there.

A few days later, Sissy stopped at the Ridge house to see Nelle. Her friend was doing the laundry. Sissy helped her hang up the wet shirts and dresses. "Are you going back to school when it starts?" she asked.

Nelle shook her head. "I don't know. Pa hasn't made up his mind." She shrugged. "Maybe it doesn't make any difference.

Why do I need school if I'm just going to get married?"

"That's what people expect of girls."

Nelle reached for a wet shirt. "Don't you dare quit school, Sissy. You have a chance for something different. I either have to live with Pa and work at the restaurant all my life or get married. That's not much of a choice. But it doesn't matter. I never liked school much, anyway." Nelle began to cry.

Sissy knew Nelle didn't mean what she said. Nelle loved school. Sissy took the shirt from her and hung it up, then led her friend to a pair of stumps so they could sit down.

"Oh, Sissy, I hate my life."

"I'm sorry," Sissy said. "Can't you do something about it?"

"Like what?"

"You could run away."

"Where would we go? How would Essie and I survive? We don't have any relatives. Besides, Pa would find us."

12

ONE AFTERNOON WHEN SISSY WAS returning from visiting Jack, she saw a woman walking down the street away from her house. She didn't pay much attention because she was thinking about Jack. She thought he had begun to improve. It looked like his leg would heal, although Doc worried about any lingering effects from the concussion. When Sissy went inside, Greenie said, "Oh, I wished you'd come home sooner. That was Mrs. Ogden. She's a friend of mine." Greenie had lots of friends, and they often had tea with her in the hour between her finishing housework and starting dinner.

"I don't know her," Sissy said.

"No, you don't, but you will before long. Well, I hope so."

Sissy didn't understand. "Are there any cookies?"

"Snickerdoodles. They're still warm." Greenie picked up the used teacups and put them into the sink below the pump. "Come and sit down. I want to talk to you."

Sissy put two cookies on a plate and another into her mouth. She spilled crumbs on the counter, then scooped them up and threw them into the garbage pail. She took the pitcher of milk out of the icebox and poured a glass, then carried everything to the table and sat down.

"Mrs. Ogden is the housekeeper at the Gilpin house," Greenie began.

Sissy's ears perked up. "Mr. Gilpin? I like him. I bet he has a wonderful house."

"I suppose he does, and before long, you just might see it close up."

Sissy put down her glass of milk and leaned forward to hear what Greenie had to say.

"The Gilpins have a boy who's nine or ten. He doesn't go to school. He's been taught at home by a tutor, but she quit, and the Gilpins have to find another. In the meantime, they want somebody who can teach the boy two days a week. Mr.

Gilpin suggested you. It seems he's impressed by how you've kept him up to date on Jack."

Sissy gulped. "Me? I don't know how to teach anybody."

"You could try. They will pay you, of course. Think how much you could add to your college money." Greenie leaned forward, too. "Maybe I shouldn't have, but I accepted for you. If you and Doc approve, of course."

Sissy thought that over. "Do you really think I could teach?"

"I *know* you can. You can do anything you set your mind to. Just look at how much you've learned from working with your father."

That night at supper, Sissy asked Doc what he thought about the tutoring job. "It would be a good experience for you," he said. "I think you should try it. Maybe you'll want to be a teacher one day."

"Don't you need me in the surgery?"

Doc shrugged. "You'd be at the Gilpin house on Wednesdays and Saturdays. I think I could manage those two days alone. In a pinch, Mrs. Greenway could help me."

Sissy didn't like the idea of adding to Greenie's work, but she still wanted to learn more about the Gilpin job. It might be fun to be a teacher. After all, she knew she wanted to do something that helped people. And teaching might be a way to leave Tenmile.

13

ON SATURDAY MORNING, AFTER SHE stopped to visit Jack, Sissy set out for the Gilpin house. It was on the mountain on the south side of Tenmile, across the valley from the Yellowcat and high above Chicken Flats. It was far away from the noise and fumes of the mine and mill.

The day before, it had rained hard, and the roads were slippery with mud. Smoke from mining operations and Chicken Flats cookstoves hovered over the town. Still, Sissy saw summer wildflowers and bluebirds like fallen bits of sky as she climbed the hill to where the Yellowcat owner lived. The Gilpin house was the biggest and nicest in town.

Sissy had seen it on the mountainside, shining in the sun like white marble, but she'd never been close. Now, standing right in front of it, she stared in awe. It was three stories high with a two-story porch on two sides. The porch and eaves were decorated with gingerbread trim. Behind the house was a stable the size of Sissy's home.

Sissy took a deep breath and knocked on the front door.

A woman opened it. Sissy assumed she must be Mrs. Gilpin. She wore a silk gown covered with lace and fringe and a necklace with a bright red stone. *Why, she looks better than ten dollars*, Sissy thought.

The woman frowned at her. "You may come in through the front door this one time," she said in a sharp voice. "From now on, however, you must use the back door, like the other employees."

"Yes, ma'am," Sissy said, biting her lip as she stepped inside. She thought Mrs. Gilpin was awfully prim.

"You are the doctor's daughter," Mrs. Gilpin said.

"Yes, ma'am."

"I assume that means you have decent manners and know the importance of cleanliness. I told Ogden I did not want a girl from a mining family." She turned up her nose a little.

Sissy thought that was a rude thing to say. Those families Mrs. Gilpin implied were dirty were the ones who kept the mine going. They made it possible for the Gilpins to have their fine house. Maybe this wasn't going to be such a great job. Sissy thought about turning around and walking back down the mountain, but Greenie would be disappointed and embarrassed.

Mrs. Gilpin left to fetch the housekeeper, and Sissy took the opportunity to look around. The entrance hall was as big as some of the houses in Chicken Flats. A wide stairway curved up to the second floor and then the third. A stained glass window set in the roof sent colored light cascading down the stairs. On one side of the hall was a dining room with a long table. Sissy counted twelve chairs. There were two parlors on the other side. The furniture was carved and looked uncomfortable. On the floor were thick rugs with bright designs. Velvet drapes hung in the doorways. Sissy ran her hand over one. The velvet was rich and soft, but it was covered with dust. Dust covered everything in a mining town, not only in the miners' cottages in Chicken Flats but in the mine owner's house, too. Sissy held back a smile. *Serves you right*, she thought.

After a couple of minutes, Mrs. Gilpin returned with the woman Sissy had seen leaving her house. "Ogden here will tell you your duties," Mrs. Gilpin said. She went into the front parlor and began to fuss with a fern that sat on a stand near the window.

"Come along," the housekeeper said. "I'm Mrs. Ogden." When Sissy looked confused, the housekeeper added quietly, "Oh, she calls me Ogden. She's from back east. I think women there call their employees by their last names. I don't mind. She's pleased you'll be working here. I heard her tell one of her friends that she was fortunate to engage the doctor's daughter."

Mrs. Ogden led Sissy into the kitchen. A plate of cinnamon rolls left over from breakfast sat on the table. "Help yourself," the housekeeper said. "I'll get you a glass of milk. Then I'll tell you your duties."

Mrs. Ogden went to the icebox and took out a pitcher. She poured milk into a glass and set it on the table, along with a fork. Then she sat down next to Sissy.

"You're to keep Master William company and help him with his lessons. It won't be easy. Miss High quit."

"Who?"

been two this year, and who knows when the Gilpins will get another. Master William slapped her, and she said she wouldn't stand for it. I don't blame her. He's a handful."

"He hit his teacher?" Sissy was horrified. "Was she hurt?"

"No, he's only nine and doesn't have any strength to speak of. I don't think it was much of a slap, but the governess had had enough. Master William is rude and often yells and refuses to do his lessons."

"He doesn't sound very nice," Sissy said.

Mrs. Ogden glanced at the door, then lowered her voice even more. "Master William can be a nice boy, but sometimes he is difficult. Miss High couldn't deal with him."

"Well, I won't let him slap *me!*"

"No, I wouldn't worry about that. That was the only time he did such a thing. But he's an angry child, which makes him misbehave. Master William gets upset over the smallest little thing."

"Why do you call him Master William?"

Mrs. Ogden laughed a little. "Mrs. Gilpin insists on it. His father calls him Willie, but we're not allowed to."

"It sounds like she thinks she's better than you," Sissy said. Greenie always said that nobody was better than anybody else—everyone was the same. "She doesn't sound very nice, either."

Mrs. Ogden took a deep breath and leaned forward, her voice soft. "She used to be. I suppose Mrs. Greenway told you all about it, so I'm not telling tales."

Sissy nodded, pretending she knew what Mrs. Ogden was talking about. Greenie hadn't said anything about Mrs. Gilpin, though.

Sissy realized she had forgotten the cinnamon roll. She picked up her fork and took a bite. The roll was good, and Sissy hoped she'd also be provided with a midday meal. She hadn't thought to bring a dinner bucket. "Oh, sure," she said, prodding Mrs. Ogden to talk.

"She used to be a very kind woman, but there has been tragedy in this house. Maybe you remember the scarlet fever epidemic two or three years back."

Sissy knew that scarlet fever was an inflammation of the nose, throat, and mouth. Its name came from the red rash that accompanied it. Doc had had several patients who were sick with it. Two of them had even died.

"Master William's older brother died from scarlet fever," Mrs. Ogden continued. "Master William caught it, too. His sickness and the older boy's death changed Mrs. Gilpin. She used to be so happy, but now she barely smiles. It makes me sad to see how she suffers." The housekeeper leaned over and whispered, "I feel sorry for her."

"But Master William lived," Sissy said.

"Yes, but she's scared to death something else will happen to him. She's spoiled him so much that he's turned into a very unpleasant boy."

"Well, I didn't even know the Gilpins had children. I wonder if I've ever seen him."

"Probably not. Mrs. Gilpin keeps a tight rein on William. She won't let him go to the local school, and she doesn't let him play outside. He spends most of his time in his room. It's almost as if he's an invalid," Mrs. Ogden explained.

Sissy was intrigued. The boy sounded mysterious. "What's wrong with him?"

Mrs. Ogden shrugged. "Who knows."

"Has my father ever been to see him?"

"Yes. Doc said all the boy needed was to get outdoors and play. Mrs. Gilpin told Doc he didn't know what he was talking about. Now he sees a specialist from Denver who comes three or four times a year. That doctor says Master

William needs rest and medicines. If you ask me, he's the one who doesn't know what he's talking about." Mrs. Ogden leaned back in her chair. "He charges a fortune, and all he does is come in here and tell me Master William needs to be kept warmer." Mrs. Ogden clucked her tongue. "Even I know that what that boy needs is fresh air. That Denver doctor is so self-important, you'd think he was the king of England." She frowned. "I shouldn't talk so, but I know you won't repeat any of this. Mrs. Greenway assured me you don't gossip."

Sissy had eaten her roll and was finishing her milk when a harsh sound came from a board on the wall.

"That's Master William now," Mrs. Ogden said. She pointed to the board. "He pushes a button when he needs something, and it rings here in the kitchen. He pushes it all the time. I'm glad you'll be with him today so I can get my work done." She sighed. "I might as well take you up to meet him. Now, remember, don't call him Willie."

Sissy started for the front hall, but Mrs. Ogden said, "This way. We use the back stairs."

"Two sets of stairs?" Sissy asked. She'd never seen a house with two staircases.

"This one is for the servants," Mrs. Ogden said. She started up the steep, narrow stairs. "Cook and I use the front staircase when Mrs. Gilpin is away," Mrs. Ogden continued.

"She has a cook?"

"And a hired girl who comes in three or four days a week, whenever Mrs. Gilpin needs her. She cleans and does the laundry. There are three of us. Four counting the coachman, who also keeps up the yard, and five when there's a governess."

Sissy wondered how much money the mine owner made if he could afford all those people to do his work. She thought of the miners like Jack's father in Chicken Flats. They worked long hours but still barely brought home enough to support their families. Many of the wives took in laundry or found other ways to make ends meet.

When they reached the second floor, Mrs. Ogden nodded at one of the closed doors. "That's where the Gilpins sleep. Those"—she indicated two other doors—"are for guests. There are more rooms on the third floor for the governess and me and one in the stable for the coachman. And Master William is in here." She pointed to a room with an open door.

"Well, it took you long enough, Ogden," a whiny voice

said as Mrs. Ogden stepped through the doorway.

Sissy followed the housekeeper into the large room. A fire burned in the fireplace. The single window was shut, and the room was hot and stuffy. And dark—at first, Sissy didn't even see the boy. Then she spotted him in bed. He had dark hair and big dark eyes, and his face was pale.

Mrs. Ogden ignored the complaint. "You haven't eaten your breakfast, Master William."

"That's because you forgot the strawberry jam. How can you expect me to eat toast without strawberry jam?" The boy was about to say something else when he spotted Sissy. "Who are you?"

"This is Sissy Carlson. She's your new tutor."

William looked Sissy up and down. "You don't look like a tutor."

"I'm new," Sissy said, hoping her voice had some authority in it.

Mrs. Ogden picked up the breakfast tray. "I'll leave you two to get acquainted." She closed the door with her foot on the way out.

Sissy went to the window and pushed back the curtains to let more light into the room. She studied the boy for a moment. He stared back, his top lip curled. "What are you looking at?"

Sissy didn't answer. Instead, she asked, "How come you're shut up in this room?"

"None of your business."

Sissy shrugged. Her first impression was right. He wasn't very nice. "How about we start on your lessons," she said.

"I hate lessons."

"I could help you with arithmetic." It was one of Sissy's best subjects.

"I told you I hate lessons. I hate arithmetic most of all." William folded his arms and frowned. Then he pointed to a box on the floor. "Get me my soldiers. You are to do what I say."

"I will if you ask politely." Sissy waited, but William didn't say anything. So she sighed and picked up the box of soldiers.

The box held two sets of metal soldiers, one in red uniforms, the other in blue. Sissy took both sets out and put them on the table.

"We'll play war," the boy said. He got out of bed and sat at the table in his nightshirt.

"Do you want red or blue, Willie?" Sissy asked.

"Red. And you must call me Master William, like the rest of the servants. It's not like you're my friend or anything. My mother wouldn't like it if you called me Willie."

Sissy thought that was a sad thing to say. How could she call a nine-year-old boy such a formal name? It was ridiculous. She bit her lip and didn't reply. Her lip was going to be awfully sore before the day was over.

William lined up the red soldiers. Sissy set up the blue ones across from them. There were twelve of each.

"I'm going to fire a cannon at you," the boy said. He knocked down two of Sissy's soldiers.

"I had twelve soldiers, and you took away two. How many do I have left?" Sissy asked.

"Ten. Everybody knows that."

"Now it's my turn to fire." She knocked over one of his soldiers. "How many are wounded all together?"

"Three."

The two continued their battle, and each time, Sissy asked how many soldiers were left. "What if you could double the number of soldiers you have? How many would that be?" she asked.

William had six soldiers left. "Twelve," he said.

"And I've got only four. What if I doubled mine?"

"Eight."

"So how many would that be all together?"

He paused to think about that. "I think it's twenty."

"Exactly right."

They continued the battle until all of Sissy's soldiers were down. "See, it's more fun to play soldiers than to do lessons," William said.

"But you just did a lesson. You did an arithmetic lesson," Sissy said.

"You tricked me. I don't like to be tricked." William tried to look stern, but Sissy could see the trace of a smile.

She grinned at him. "You're not as mean as you think you are," she said.

Mrs. Ogden brought up a tray. "Mrs. Gilpin is pleased with how things are going. She is entertaining friends for luncheon, as she calls it, and you haven't called for her once, Master William." Sissy wondered if Mrs. Gilpin really cared about her teaching William. Maybe she only cared that Sissy kept the boy occupied so he wouldn't bother her.

After the two had eaten, Sissy read to William. "Now it's your turn to read to me."

"I don't want to. That's a schoolbook. It's so boring."

"It's the only book here."

"No, it isn't." William went to a window seat, opened the lid, and took out a children's book. It was a story about a boy who was an explorer in foreign lands. "I like this one, but Miss High wouldn't let me read it. She said novels were bad for my brain."

"Well, I don't think so. I've read this one. It's a good book. Do you want to read it out loud to me?"

"Mother said I shouldn't read it if Miss High didn't approve. Will you tell on me?"

Sissy shook her head. "Not if you don't tell on me. I think it's a fun book." Sissy guessed Mrs. Gilpin probably wouldn't agree, but the woman hadn't come upstairs all afternoon.

William considered that. Then he grinned. "I know, one of my puppets can read it." He pointed at a toy theater set up on the floor. Half a dozen puppets were slumped on the stage. "Get the clown. If Mother asks if I read this book, I can tell her no, because the clown read it."

"I think that would work." Sissy picked up the puppet and handed it to William.

He opened the book and began to read in a laughing voice. After a few minutes, he asked for the girl puppet with the long, braided hair. He read in a high-pitched voice that made them both giggle. Using all kinds of phony voices, he read for almost an hour, until Mrs. Ogden came up to tell Sissy it was time for her to go home.

"When are you coming back?" William asked.

"Wednesday. We can play soldiers again. But I expect you to be dressed when I get here."

"Okay." William grinned. As Sissy started for the door, the boy called, "Sissy."

"Yes?"

"When we're alone, you can call me Willie."

"Okay. Tap 'er light, Willie."

"What does that mean?"

"It's what the miners say. It means take it easy."

"Okay. Tap 'er light, Sissy."

14

SINCE IT WAS NEARLY FALL now, mushroom season was waning, but there were still good mushrooms to be found in the high country. Greenie had gone out by herself several times to hunt for them. Still, the big jar where she kept dried porcini and meadow mushrooms was not yet full. She wanted to fill it up so she would have enough for winter cooking.

"Come along," she told Sissy one day as she got out her wicker basket. "We'll take Nelle with us again. She needs a break."

Sissy and Doc hadn't been back to Delmonico's since

the night Essie had dropped the tray of dishes more than a month before. Now that she knew how Mr. Ridge treated his daughters, Sissy didn't care to see him. Still, when she went to Chicken Flats to visit Jack, Sissy often stopped to see Nelle, too. Nelle was always glad for a visit. She needed someone to talk to. "You keep up my spirits," she told Sissy.

Mushrooming will keep up Nelle's spirits, too, Sissy thought as she hurried to her friend's house.

Nelle was hanging up the wash when Sissy got there. "Want to go mushrooming?" she asked.

"I have to finish the wash first."

"I'll help."

Sissy picked up the corner of a tablecloth and pinned it to the clothesline. Just then, the door banged open, and Mr. Ridge came outside.

"Haven't you finished?" he yelled. "Are you wasting time? I can give you something else to—" He stopped when he saw Sissy. "Well, look who's here! It's Doc Carlson's pretty little girl. When are you going to come to Delmonico's for another piece of coconut cake?"

"Hi, Mr. Ridge," Sissy said, pretending she hadn't heard him yell. "Doc's been awful busy, so we haven't gone out much. And Mrs. Greenway is a good cook."

"You'll hurt Nelle's feelings if you don't stop by."

"Yes, sir. I came to see if Nelle could go mushrooming with us."

Mr. Ridge thought that over. "I'll tell you what. I'll trade you a piece of coconut cake for a basket of mushrooms."

That a lot of work for just one piece of cake, Sissy thought.

When Sissy didn't answer, Mr. Ridge said, "I expect she can go, but she has to finish hanging up the wash first."

When Sissy returned with Nelle, Greenie smiled. "I hoped you'd come. I fixed a special lunch."

Nelle grinned, then grew sad. "I wish that Jack could come, too. Remember, he went with us once last summer? Do you think he'll be well enough next year?"

"I hope so," Sissy said. She thought of how Jack had spotted the most mushrooms and filled his basket first.

The late summer day was beautiful. Purple asters bloomed along the trail up the mountain. The aspen had begun to turn colors. They spilled their leaves like gold coins across the ground. There was a dusting of snow on the highest mountains, and it was chilly under the tall pines. The mushrooms weren't as plentiful as they had been earlier in the summer. Greenie and the two girls had to look over each mushroom carefully before they put it into a basket. Some were old and dried up, and others had bugs. It seemed to Sissy that they threw away as many as they kept.

Still, it was fun spotting them. Sissy's favorites were the umbrella-shaped porcini mushrooms with round brown tops like caps of silk. She found a clump of them in the shade of a rotten log. She gave Nelle half.

"You found them. You ought to give them to Mrs. Greenway," Nelle said.

"Oh, keep them. I have more than the two of you put together," Greenie said.

Sissy looked at the three baskets and, realizing Greenie was right, decided she'd give all her mushrooms to Nelle when they were done. *Mr. Ridge would be pleased, and maybe he wouldn't yell at Nelle so much today*, she thought.

When the sun was high, they stopped in the shade of an aspen grove. Greenie unpacked a lunch from the knapsack on her back. She spread it out on a stump. There were ham sandwiches and deviled eggs and Greenie's special cookies with pockets of raspberry jam in the center. Greenie had even brought along a bottle of lemonade.

"Oh boy, ham," Nelle said.

"Aren't you tired of it? I'd think you'd have it every night since it's your specialty at the restaurant," Sissy said.

"It's usually gone by the time we eat. We eat leftovers," Nelle said. She added quickly, "But they're awful good leftovers."

The three ate in silence. When they were finished, Nelle leaned back against a white aspen trunk and closed her eyes. The dappled sunlight made a pattern on her face. "I could stay here all day," she said.

"You girls enjoy the mountains now while you can. It won't be long before school starts," Greenie told them.

Nelle sat up and sighed. She started to say something but began crying instead.

"What's wrong?" Sissy asked.

Nelle shook her head. "I'm sorry. It's not your problem."

"What is it?" Greenie took Nelle's hand. "You can tell us, dear. Both Sissy and I are your friends."

"It's my father."

"Did he hurt you?" Sissy asked. "Or Essie?"

"It's not that." Nelle shook her head. "I can't go to school anymore. It's definite."

"Why?" Greenie asked. She poured the rest of the lemonade into Nelle's tin cup. "Your father?"

Nelle nodded.

Greenie pursed her lips in anger. "He won't let you go?"

"He says someone has to help full-time in the restaurant. One of us will have to quit school and work for him."

"But Essie's only in fourth grade," Sissy said. She looked at Greenie, whose hands were clenched into fists. She'd never seen Greenie so angry.

Nelle picked up a handful of fallen aspen leaves and let them sift through her hands. "That's just it. If I stay in school, Essie has to quit. If I leave, Essie can stay. Oh, Sissy, I knew this would happen. Still, I prayed I'd at least graduate from eighth grade." She put her hands over her face as she started to cry again. "I even dreamed of finishing high school so I'd have enough education to leave here and get a job. Then I wouldn't have to work at the restaurant with Pa all my life. Now the only other choice I have is to get married someday."

"You want to leave Tenmile?" Greenie asked. She

gathered up the remains of their lunch and packed them in her knapsack.

"More than anything. Essie and I talk about it all the time. I was going to finish high school. Then I was going to go to Denver or Colorado Springs or Pueblo—anywhere but Tenmile—and find a job. I was planning to take Essie with me so she could finish school there."

"Would your father let you go?" Sissy asked. She stood and brushed off her skirt.

"No, of course not. We'd have to just leave. But we can't do that if I don't have an education. Who would pay me enough money to support both Essie and me now?"

"Could you go by yourself? Maybe you can get a job as a waitress. You already know how to do that," Sissy said.

"Then Essie would be alone with Pa. I'd never abandon her."

Greenie stood and slung the knapsack onto her back. "School won't start for several weeks yet. Maybe we can think of something by then."

Nelle wiped her face and smiled. "That's nice of you to say, Mrs. Greenway. But there isn't anything anybody can do. Maybe school isn't so important, anyway." She picked up her basket. "Now, I'm going to fill this basket with mushrooms, and I'm not going home until I do!"

As Nelle started off ahead of them, Greenie took Sissy's hand and squeezed it. "I know you're upset. We'll do what we can."

15

Sissy, Greenie, and Nelle had more success hunting for mushrooms after their picnic. They spotted them beside fallen logs and in patches of kinnikinic, tiny green leaves with bright red berries. They made their way up the trail until they reached the Washington cabin. Sarah came out the door holding her doll and waved. "Mama, folks is come," she called behind her.

Willow Louise appeared in the doorway, her feet bare. She put her hand to her forehead to block out the sun, then recognized Greenie.

"You'uns are right welcome," she said. Sarah grinned.

The feather Sissy had given her was once more in her braid, though it was now tattered.

"Hi, Willow Louise. Hi, Sarah," Sissy called. "I brought my friend Nelle. Remember her?"

"I'm glad to see you. I been lonesome for outside company since my man's been laid up."

"What's wrong?" Sissy asked.

"He hurts more than two dollars. He's got a rising in his head. It plagues him. Might be it's the ague."

Sissy knew that ague was a fever with chills and sweating. "Does he have an appetite?"

She shook her head. "I fried him up some bread, but he can't seem to take it."

"He ought to see my father. He's a doctor."

"Oh, Eual—that's my husband—he don't hold with doctors none."

Sissy had heard people say that before. Sometimes it meant they couldn't pay.

"What have you done for him?" Greenie asked.

"I put seven buttons on a string and tied it around his neck, but it didn't do nothing."

Sissy and Greenie exchanged a glance. They knew that

some folk remedies worked. In fact, Doc sometimes used them. But a string of buttons wasn't going to do anything.

"Sissy here could take a look at him," Greenie said.

Willow Louise frowned. "What's she know?"

"She helps her father."

"She's a girl."

"It wouldn't hurt," Greenie told Willow Louise. "Sissy's a healer."

The woman thought that over. "I knowed a woman back home that was a healer." She turned to look inside the cabin door, then said, "No, I guess it wouldn't hurt none."

Sissy glanced up at Greenie. She'd never examined anybody by herself. She'd always been at Doc's side. She wasn't sure she should do this. Doc might not approve. Still, maybe Greenie was right—it wouldn't do any harm. She could report back to her father if the man was really sick.

"Go on," Greenie said. "You'll do fine."

While Nelle played with Sarah and Betsy in the yard, Sissy followed Willow Louise inside. The cabin was tidy, but it was dark. A fire burned in a small stone fireplace along one wall. A man rested on a pad of quilts laid on pine branches on the dirt floor. The air felt damp, and Sissy shivered a little.

"Eual, this here's the doc's daughter. She's a healer, too. She'll take a look at you," Willow Louise said. She lit a kerosene lamp and held it over her husband. Sissy could see that his face was pale and he was shaking.

She went closer and reached out a hand to touch the man's forehead. It was hot. Although he was shivering with cold, he had a fever. She felt his wrist for a pulse. It was fast.

Someone with ague had come to Doc just the week before. Doc had talked as he'd treated the man, and Sissy tried to remember what her father had said. "I think he needs quinine," Sissy told Greenie. "And sulfuric acid." She asked Willow Louise, "Do you have anything like that?"

Willow Louise shook her head. "I don't know what that it, but I know we don't got it. We got nothing for medicine."

Sissy tried to remember if she had read anything about ague in Greenie's all-purpose household book, *Dr. Chase's Recipes: Or, Information For Everybody*. "Do you have any eggs?"

Willow Louise grinned. "We do. I keep three chickens."

Sissy went to the fireplace and scraped some soot off the chimney. "I read you could mix this with a little water and an egg and sugar. Your husband should drink it. I think it might work."

Willow Louise cracked an egg into a dish while Sissy collected more soot from the fireplace. Adding it to the dish along with a pinch of sugar and some water, Sissy mixed up the concoction. She poured it into a tin cup and handed it to Eual. He made a face when he sipped it.

"Tastes like mine runoff. I purely can't drink it."

"You finish it, Mr. Washington. It'll help you," Sissy ordered. She tried to sound like her father when he told a patient to drink something nasty.

Eual made a face, but he drank the mixture.

"Now we have to get him outside. It's too damp and cold in here. He should lie in the sun all day long," Sissy said when he handed her the empty cup.

After Eual went to sleep outside, Willow Louise told Sissy, "I'll thank you till you're better paid."

Sissy shook her head. She knew now why her father didn't hound people to pay him. She liked the feeling of helping someone.

Because of the mountains, darkness came early to the Tenmile Range. By the time Sissy and Greenie left the Washingtons' cabin, the sun had almost slipped behind the high peaks. Long shadows covered the trail back down to town. Nelle had gone on ahead so she wouldn't be late to the restaurant. Now, as she hurried along with Sissy, Greenie said, "You did a good job back there. Maybe you should think about being a doctor."

"I've already thought about that, Greenie. Girls can't be doctors. Papa said so."

"Well, I don't know why not."

Sissy thought that over. Why not, indeed? She turned and waved at Willow Louise. "Do you think Eual will come to see Papa if he doesn't get better?"

"I doubt it," Greenie replied. "They can't pay, and they wouldn't want to be beholden. They're fierce with pride."

That night, Sissy told Doc how she had treated Eual Washington. She thought he would be proud of her.

Instead, he said, "You shouldn't have done that, Sissy.

You're not a doctor."

"Greenie says maybe I could be one."

Doc gave a bark of a laugh. "You're a girl. Maybe you could be a nurse. But you still shouldn't have done what you did."

Early one morning a few days later, Sissy heard a knock on the back door. She opened it to find Sarah standing there.

"Pa's well," she said. "Ma'd send you a letter, but she can't handwrite." Sarah held out a basket made of willow twigs. It was filled with wild raspberries. Before Sissy could thank her, the little girl turned and ran, her bare feet padding softly on the dirt street.

Doc was sitting at the table eating breakfast as he read the newspaper. He looked up. "What was that all about?"

"Mr. Washington, the prospector with ague who I helped in the mountains—he's well. They sent us these raspberries," Sissy said. "Maybe what I did cured him." She held her breath, waiting to see what Doc would say.

"Or maybe he didn't have ague after all," Doc told her.

He began reading the paper again and did not see Sissy's face fall. "Oh, by the way," he said, turning a page, "Tincup Charlie came by yesterday and paid me the dollar he owed for extracting his tooth."

16

JUST BEFORE SCHOOL STARTED, SISSY went to visit Jack again. He was lying in a bed his father had set up for him in their front room. It had been more than a month since his accident, and Sissy thought he looked healthier.

"I feel stronger," Jack said. "You think I'm going to be okay? Doc was here last week, but he wouldn't tell me anything."

If Doc hadn't said anything, Sissy didn't dare to, either. "I don't know. It can take a while to heal from such bad injuries. But I'm glad you feel better."

Jack grinned at her. "Maybe I ought to get some books and study while I'm in bed."

"That's a good idea. I'll bring them to you."

"Thanks, Sissy. I like it when you come to see me. Mr. Gilpin visited once. Doc is here a lot, and the boys from school. But it's best when you come."

Sissy squeezed his arm. "After school starts, I'll still come as often as I can."

When Sissy left the house, Mrs. Burke followed her outside to the porch, saying, "We're hopeful, more than we've been before, although Doc says we have to give him time."

"Doc knows best," Sissy replied. "I'm going to bring some schoolbooks so Jack can study."

Mrs. Burke smiled. "Maybe we can find a way for Jack to go back to school. He is our hope." She went back inside and closed the door.

Peter was sitting on a bench on the porch. Sissy sat down beside him. "When Mr. Gilpin was here, I heard him say you're working for him," Peter said.

"I'm Willie's tutor, which means I teach him lessons. I go twice a week. Do you know him?"

"Yeah, I remember Willie. We were friends once. He let me use his sled. It was new. His pa bought it for him. I crashed it. I thought Willie would be mad, but he wasn't. He said it was only bent a little and now he didn't have to worry about being careful with it." Peter laughed.

"Did you like him?"

"He was swell," Peter said. "Once we were racing by his house, and I fell and skinned my leg. Willie took me home. His ma cleaned me up. Then she made us hot chocolate. I never had hot chocolate before. She was nice, too. Then Willie got sick. I haven't seen him in a couple of years." Peter raised his pants leg a little and pointed to a scar. "That's where I got hurt. After Arthur died, I tried to see Willie. I went to his house. Mrs. Gilpin always told me he was busy. I don't think she likes me anymore, and after a while I gave up. What's Willie like now?"

"Spoiled. Lonely." Sissy winced. She worked for the Gilpins and shouldn't have said that about Willie.

"I bet his ma doesn't like me because I live in Chicken Flats."

"Well, I bet Willie likes you no matter where you live."

The following Wednesday, Sissy knocked on the back door

of the Gilpin house. Mrs. Ogden opened it. "I'm glad you're here." She lowered her voice. "Master William has been a horror all day. The missus keeps asking when you'll get here. She's entertaining her friends and is about to tear her hair out. She wants you to keep Master William busy in his room."

The buzzer on the wall sounded, and Mrs. Ogden sighed. "That's the fourth time this morning. I'm worn out just from going up and down the stairs."

Sissy said in a low voice, "Last time I was here, Mrs. Gilpin heard me call Master William Willie. She jumped all over me."

Mrs. Ogden said, "Don't let her get to you. She has some strange ideas about how to treat the people who work for her. She doesn't want us to get uppity. Her bark is worse than her bite, though. Now Mr. Gilpin's another thing. He doesn't hold with all this fancy living. I think he'd just as soon eat in the kitchen with the help. You go on up and see to *Master* William. Get him out from under me," Mrs. Ogden said.

Sissy started for the back stairs. Just then, a girl came down the staircase and into the kitchen.

"Emma!" Sissy said.

The girl looked Sissy up and down. She did not seem

pleased to see her. "So *you're* the new tutor. I could do that. I know just as much as you do. But I guess I'm not as good as the *doctor's* daughter."

Sissy was taken aback. She and Emma used to be school friends. "What are you doing here?" she asked.

"I *work* here," Emma said.

Sissy remembered then that Mrs. Ogden had told her a maid came in several times a week, but she hadn't said the maid's name. Apparently, Emma and Sissy usually worked on different days, and that was why they hadn't run into each other before. Sissy recalled that Emma's father had been killed and she'd had to drop out of school. Emma and her older brother had taken jobs to help support their younger brothers and sisters. Emma, Sissy now realized, had become a maid. She had been friendly enough in school, but now she seemed angry and bitter. Sissy couldn't blame her. It didn't seem like Emma had an easy life. Her circumstances had changed since Sissy had seen her last.

"I didn't mean to take your job," Sissy said. "I didn't know."

"Oh, you didn't take Emma's job," Mrs. Ogden put in. "You were the only one the Gilpins considered hiring as a tutor."

Sissy remembered that Mrs. Gilpin had said she didn't want a girl from Chicken Flats.

As if she knew what Sissy was thinking, Emma snarled, "She thinks I'm not good enough. All I'm good for is cleaning her house."

Mrs. Ogden stepped in. "Now, Emma. This is not Sissy's fault. You go on about your business. Sissy has to see to Master William."

Emma glared at Sissy. "Yeah, you go see to the brat."

"He's not a brat!" Sissy said.

"That's what you think. He threw his glass of milk at me. I came downstairs to get a rag to mop it up. I guess that's *your* job now." Emma went into the pantry and slammed the door.

Sissy turned to Mrs. Ogden with a questioning look.

Mrs. Ogden shrugged. "Don't let her get to you. Things are hard for her. She told me she wanted to be a teacher. You know how it is in Tenmile. Girls quit school and work themselves to the bone to support their families. Then they marry and do the same work at home as wives. I'd be angry, too, if that was all I had to look forward to."

Sissy stared at the pantry door. She felt sorry for Emma,

but she was wary. Yet what could she do?

The buzzer on the wall sounded again. Sissy hurried up the back stairs with a rag in her hand. Willie was sitting on the floor, his back to her.

"You sure are slow. Take my breakfast tray away."

"Hi, Willie," Sissy said.

"You are not to call me—" He turned around and recognized Sissy. "Oh, it's you."

"How come you threw a glass of milk at Emma?" Sissy asked.

Willie didn't answer at first. He just stared at Sissy as she wiped up the spill on the floor. "I don't like her. She's always mad."

"I guess you'd be mad, too, if you had to quit school to go to work."

"Then she shouldn't have done it."

Sissy set the wet rag in a basin on the dresser. "She didn't have any choice. Her father was killed."

Willie ran his finger over a design in the rug he was sitting on. "Her brother could have gone to work, then."

"He did. I think he works in the Yellowcat, but he probably doesn't make enough to support the family. There are five or six little kids at home."

"Well, that's not my fault."

No, Sissy thought, *but maybe it's your father's fault. Maybe he ought to pay the mine workers higher wages.*

"Get my soldiers," Willie said.

Sissy put her hands on her hips. "Do you think you could say please?"

"I don't have to. You work for me."

"I work for your mother."

Willie looked down at the carpet. He said in a low voice, "Okay. Please."

"Of course," Sissy told him. "But would you rather play checkers?" She had seen a checkerboard among Willie's toys.

"Will you turn that into another arithmetic lesson?" He glared at Sissy.

"You bet." Sissy grinned.

Willie's glare turned into a smile. "Okay. But only if I get to be in charge of addition."

"Deal!" Sissy took out the checkerboard and set it up on the bed. "Red or black?"

"Red."

Sissy placed the checkers on the board.

"I get to make up the rules, too," Willie said. "Reds are one point. Blacks are two. So if I take one of your black checkers, I get two points."

"But I get only one point if I take one of yours? That's not fair."

"You agreed I could be in charge."

"You're tricky."

They both burst out laughing.

At that moment, Mrs. Gilpin came into the room. She stared at the two children. Sissy wondered if she'd be angry that they were playing checkers instead of doing lessons. "Why are you laughing?" she asked.

"Because I'm going to beat Sissy at checkers," he explained.

Mrs. Gilpin smiled. Sissy had never seen her smile. "Don't forget you have lessons to do. Sissy isn't here to play."

"But this is a lesson. Sissy says it's an arithmetic lesson," Willie insisted.

"Well, if you say so." Mrs. Gilpin looked a little bit confused as she left the room.

"Let's play! You keep score. You're the teacher."

17

SCHOOL HAD STARTED. SISSY WORKED after school on Wednesdays and all day Saturdays at the Gilpin house now. Doc agreed that she could keep the job if it didn't interfere with her studies. Mrs. Gilpin wanted her to continue working two full days every week, but Sissy pointed out that she attended school.

"Emma doesn't think it's necessary to attend school."

"Emma doesn't have any choice. She has to help support her family."

"Oh," Mrs. Gilpin said. "Well, I suppose that's true." She turned and left the room.

Sissy wondered if Mrs. Gilpin really believed that Tenmile girls quit school because they wanted to. Would she have even given it another thought if Sissy hadn't said something?

Between tutoring Willie and going to school, Sissy had less time to see Jack and Nelle. She could see Jack whenever she was free, but Nelle always seemed to be at the restaurant with her father, and he didn't like Sissy interrupting her work.

One afternoon when she didn't have to be at the Gilpin house, she stopped by the Burkes' place with an armload of schoolbooks. Jack was lying on the bed in the front room. His face was white, and he was tossing around. On her last visit, he'd looked as if he had really improved. He had even begun to study. Now it appeared he had taken a turn for the worse.

"Doc says my leg might have to come off. It's infected," Jack told her in a strangled voice. He pushed back the blanket so she could see the pus oozing from the wound.

"I thought you were getting better. You looked so good last time."

"I thought so, too. Doc says sometimes it happens this way. It seems like you're going to be okay, but . . ." He stopped and wiped his eyes with the back of his hand.

"Oh, Jack!" she said. "Is it really so? You might lose your leg?" Sissy was angry that Doc hadn't told her. He knew Jack was her best friend.

"Maybe. Life stinks. Now I'll never go to college and be an engineer. Heck, I won't even be a miner again." He blinked rapidly. "I'll be a cripple the rest of my life, like some no-good drunk standing in front of a saloon, begging with a tin cup."

Sissy reached out and took Jack's hand. There was a lump in her throat, and she couldn't reply. *We're so alike*, she thought. They both wanted to make something of themselves and leave Tenmile. Now Sissy still had her dream, but it felt like Jack's was slipping away. "There's plenty of work you can do," she said.

"What, in a wheelchair?" He turned away so Sissy wouldn't see him cry. "Maybe if I had an education, I could be a bookkeeper. I could even have been an engineer if this had happened *after* I went to college. But there's not a thing I can do that a man with two legs can't do better."

Sissy gripped Jack's hand. She'd never had a better friend. "You have to make it for both of us, Sissy," he said.

When Sissy left the Burke house, she went up the mountain to her private grove, where she could think. It was quiet. The mining noise was far away. The birds were gone, and the aspen trees had lost their leaves. Even the squirrel had disappeared. Sissy felt lonely. She kicked a rock with the toe of her shoe and sent it down the mountain. Then she sat down and clenched her fists. Life wasn't fair for Nelle or Jack. Both of them wanted to get away from Tenmile. But Nelle was stuck with her horrible father, and a stupid mining accident had taken away Jack's future. Now Sissy was the only one who had a chance to make something of herself, to discover the world beyond the Tenmile Range. She wondered if she would do it or if she would fail, too.

18

"Do you remember Peter Burke?" Sissy asked Willie one day. They were finished with lessons for the afternoon.

"Sure. We used to play ball and explore and go sledding. We had sword fights with icicles, too. But Pete wasn't a very good friend. He never came to see me after I got sick."

"Yes, he did—" Sissy began. She wanted to say that Peter had called several times. But it wasn't her place to tell Willie that his mother had turned away his friend. "Maybe Pete came and you didn't know it."

"No, Mother would have told me. Pete probably thought I was going to make him sick. Or maybe he decided I wouldn't be fun to play with anymore since I have to stay in the house. He probably doesn't know I got well." Then Willie smiled, remembering. "We sledded on the mine dumps. I ran into some rocks once and fell off. I knocked out my tooth. Good thing it was a baby tooth."

"Your mother must have been upset."

"No, she never got upset back then. We used to do all kinds of fun things. Father took us into the mine sometimes. I loved going down in the hole. I wanted to be an engineer, just like Father. He told me all about rocks and what to look for when you're hunting for gold. Once Pete and I found a gold nugget."

Sissy was impressed. "What did you do with it?"

"I gave it to Pete. I wonder if he still has it. Me and Pete found some swell ore samples."

"Pete and I," Sissy corrected. Willie was still seated at his desk, where they had just finished an English lesson.

"Pete and I," Willie repeated. "I'll show you. Get my box of rocks."

Sissy didn't move.

"It's over there." Willie pointed to a shelf. "Get it."

Sissy stayed where she was until Willie said, "*Please* get it."

"Sure." Sissy found a wooden box on the shelf. Inside was a collection of ore samples that the two of them spread out on the desk. Willie told her where each one had come from. He explained what type of rock each sample was and showed her the streaks of pay dirt.

"This one came out of the Yellowcat. Father gave it to me. He picked it up himself!"

Sissy had seen Mr. Gilpin in Doc's office and at the mine office when she had gone to tell him about Jack's progress, but she'd rarely seen him at home. "He must work long hours."

Willie looked away. "He didn't used to. He always had dinner with us. He'd play ball with Arthur and me and take us hiking. He doesn't have time for me now that Mother won't let me do those things. She's afraid I'll die like Arthur. That doctor who comes from Denver tells her I shouldn't exert myself. Those were his words—I heard him. Mother believes him, and when she makes up her mind about something, well, you can't change it." Willie looked down at an ore sample and ran his finger along the rough edge of the rock. "Mother and Father are going to Denver for the weekend. Father has a mining conference, and Mother wants to shop. They used to take Arthur and me, but they don't take me anymore."

"When will they be back?" Sissy asked.

"Not until Monday."

"Are you sure?"

"Yes. Father wants to see a horse race on Saturday. Mother agreed if he'd take her to a concert on Sunday. I wish I could go . . . to the horse race, anyway." He looked wistful.

"Maybe we could plan something special while they're away," Sissy said.

"What?"

"It wouldn't be special if I told you. It'll be a surprise."

19

On Saturday, Sissy entered the Gilpin house through the back door.

"The missus is in Denver. You could have used the front door," Mrs. Ogden told her. "Sometimes it makes me tired, the way she thinks she's so grand. She's lucky is all. We have to put up with it . . . but not when she's away." Then she looked behind Sissy. "What—?"

"Shhh." Sissy put a finger to her mouth. "Come on."

She started up the stairs. When she reached the second floor, she headed for Willie's room. She knocked on the door.

"Come on in," Willie called.

Sissy opened the door, then stepped aside. "Surprise!" she cried.

Peter Burke jumped out from behind her, a big grin on his face.

"Pete?" Willie yelled. "Yay, Pete!"

Peter rushed into the room and slapped Willie on the back.

Willie studied Peter. "You've grown."

"Yeah," Peter said proudly. "I'm just about the tallest boy in the class. Taller than you, I bet."

"Bet not." The two boys stood back-to-back, and Willie asked, "Who's the tallest, Sissy?"

"It's a tie. You're the same."

"Yeah, I guess we always were," Willie said. He grew serious. "Sissy told me about Jack. I'm really sorry he's sick."

Peter nodded. "Thanks. I remember when Arthur was sick, too."

The two boys looked at each other, and Sissy realized the bond they had formed as little children was still there.

"Hey, I brought my marbles. Want to play?" Peter asked.

The two boys knelt on the floor. Peter pulled his sack of marbles from his pocket. He opened it and held up a bright one. "Remember the Red Devil?" Sissy thought it glittered in the light like Mrs. Gilpin's ruby necklace.

"My best marble. You won it off me. You've still got it?" Willie asked.

"Sure thing. I'm giving you another chance. You won't win it back, though. I'm better than you are."

"Are not." Willie rummaged through his toys until he found his own marbles. He spread them on the floor. "Hey, boys, you want the Red Devil back?" he asked the brightly colored glass balls.

"Nah. You're not that good," Peter said.

"I'll show you!"

Willie tried hard, but he was no match for Peter. After he lost three marbles, he said, "Hey, that's not fair. I'm out of practice."

"Tough luck," Peter said.

Sissy grinned. Everybody felt sorry for Willie and gave in to him. It was nice to see that Peter didn't. He treated Willie as if he were just an ordinary boy.

The boys played for a long time. Willie won back one

marble, but he didn't win the Red Devil. He and Peter were putting away the marbles when they heard a loud boom from outside.

"They're blasting up on the mountain. Let's go see if we can tell where they're doing it," Peter said.

"I can't," Willie told him. "Mother doesn't let me go outside without her. She wants me to stay in my room."

Peter frowned. "That stinks." Then he got a sly look on his face. "I bet she didn't say anything about the porch. It's not *really* outside. Let's go there and watch." Peter went into the hallway, which had a door to the second-story porch.

Willie looked at Sissy for permission. She was pretty sure Mrs. Gilpin wouldn't like it if she took Willie outside. *But maybe it doesn't matter as long as she doesn't know,* Sissy thought. The fresh air would do Willie good.

"All right," she said, and followed the boys. The porch was filled with tables and chairs. The three sat down.

Since the Gilpin house was high on the mountain across from the mine, they could look directly across the valley and see the activity. They could see down into Chicken Flats, too. "I'll ask Father what they're doing up there when he gets home," Willie said.

"Um . . ." Sissy said.

Willie grinned at her. "It's okay. I'll say I heard the sound from my room. That's not a lie. I really did."

As Willie waited for more dynamite charges to go off, he studied the mountain. "The mine's gotten bigger. Look at all the new buildings around the entrance. Father didn't tell me they'd built more." He sounded disappointed. "He used to tell Arthur and me everything that was going on. He'd take out maps and explain things to us." After a time, Willie said, "Maybe he liked Arthur better than me."

"Nah," Peter said. "Remember when he took us down in the Yellowcat? Arthur didn't even want to go. He didn't care about mining." He turned to Sissy. "I was afraid to get into that bucket and ride all the way down the shaft. It was hundreds of feet to the bottom. But Willie wasn't scared. Mr. Gilpin said he'd make a good miner. He pointed out the ore vein to us."

Willie turned to Sissy. "That means the streak of gold in the rock."

Having lived in a mining town all her life, Sissy knew what an ore vein was. But she pretended she didn't since Willie was so excited to tell her.

"It was in the adit. That's like a tunnel that has just one end. We found the gold nugget there. Remember, Pete? Do you still have it?"

Peter looked away. "Oh, it's somewhere," he said.

"You better not have lost it."

Peter didn't reply.

A few minutes later, Mrs. Ogden came upstairs carrying a tray. The housekeeper was surprised to see the porch door open and the three children sitting outside. "What in the world?" she said. She looked at Sissy and raised her eyebrows.

Sissy shrugged. "The boys wanted to come out here. I didn't see any harm in it."

"I don't know," Mrs. Ogden said, shaking her head. Sissy realized she might get the housekeeper in trouble.

"I won't tell Mother, I promise," Willie said.

Mrs. Ogden looked relieved. "I can't see that mountain air ever hurt anybody," she said. She told Willie, "I brought your luncheon."

"I guess I better go," Peter said.

"Certainly not," Mrs. Ogden told him. "I brought a plate for you, too."

Peter smiled. "Wow! Is there hot chocolate?"

Mrs. Ogden glanced at Sissy. "It's in the kitchen. I couldn't bring everything up at one time."

"I'll come with you to fetch it," Sissy said. She helped Mrs. Ogden set the plates on the porch table, then followed the woman down the stairs. "Is there really any hot chocolate?" she asked.

"I think so. Nobody's asked for it in a long time. I'd hate to disappoint that little boy. I haven't seen Master William so happy since he got sick. Bringing Peter to visit was a good idea. I wish he could come more often and without sneaking around, but the missus might not like it."

She took down a bar of chocolate to grate, and then asked Sissy to get out the sugar. She heated milk on the stove.

Sissy spooned the chocolate and sugar into two cups. "I'll take the blame if she finds out. If she fires me . . ." Sissy shrugged. She enjoyed teaching Willie, but she thought it was awful that the boy didn't have anyone to play with.

As Mrs. Ogden poured hot milk into the cups, Sissy asked, "How come Mr. Gilpin doesn't pay attention to Willie? He said his father used to be with him all the time."

"That's a sad thing." Mrs. Gilpin sighed. "He was close to those boys."

"Willie thinks he liked Arthur better."

"That's not so. He loved being with Willie because the boy was interested in mining. He had plans to send Willie to the Colorado School of Mines. But now, who knows?" She shook her head. "That's years away. He ought to be well long before that."

"I don't think there's anything wrong with Willie except that he stays inside too much."

Mrs. Ogden nodded. "I know. But it's not my place—or yours either—to say anything to the Gilpins." Mrs. Ogden put the cups on a tray. "It may not seem like it, but Mrs. Gilpin loves that boy fiercely. That's why she's scared to death of losing him. She'd rather see him safe indoors for the rest of his life than let him risk getting hurt by being a regular boy."

"That's not good for him."

"You tell that to Mrs. Gilpin. I won't."

After the two boys finished their hot chocolate, Peter said, "I guess I better go."

"Thanks for coming. This is the best day I've had since I

got sick," Willie told him.

"Yeah. Sorry about the Red Devil." Peter grinned.

"Next time," Willie told him.

After Peter left, Willie said to Sissy, "Pete told me he came to see me a bunch of times. Mother wouldn't let him come in. I wonder why."

"You were sick."

"But she could have told me, couldn't she?"

Sissy shrugged.

"I bet Pete still has that gold nugget."

Sissy wasn't so sure. *I bet he gave it to his mother to buy food*, she thought.

A few days after she took Peter to visit Willie, Sissy stopped by the Burke house just as a delivery man was leaving.

"Look what we got," Peter said. "It just came." A big basket of fruit sat on the kitchen table.

Little Joe stood by the basket, his eyes wide. He reached for an apple, but Mrs. Burke shook her head. "It's a present for Jackie."

"Look, Jack," Sissy said, pointing at the basket. She'd never seen so much fruit all at once. She wondered where it had come from.

"You'll never guess who sent it," Mr. Burke said.

Sissy looked at him expectantly.

"Mr. Gilpin."

"Wow. He's rich," Peter said.

"I think it's real nice of him," Mrs. Burke said.

Sissy thought so, too, although she thought money might have been a more helpful gift.

"Wow!" Peter said. "There's a banana in there. I never saw one before except in a picture."

"That's nice." Jack was lying in bed. He didn't look strong enough to sit up. "I don't feel like eating anything. You boys can have it."

"Really?" Little Joe asked.

"Really," Jack told him as he pulled the blanket tight around himself.

Peter grabbed the banana, then whispered to Sissy, "How do you eat it?"

"I think that's a skin. You have to peel it off."

Peter broke the skin with his finger and peeled it back,

staring at the white banana inside. He ate it slowly, grinning. "When I grow up, I'm going to have a banana every day."

Sissy watched him eat it. When Peter was finished, Sissy asked, "Did Mr. Gilpin really send it?"

Peter shook his head. "I bet it was Mrs. Gilpin. I bet Willie told her to."

20

ONE WEDNESDAY WHEN SHE KNEW Mrs. Gilpin was away, Sissy stopped at the Burke house to collect Peter. Jack was in his bed in the front room. "Have you been studying those books?" Sissy asked him.

Jack nodded. "I sure have. I'm feeling much better."

Sissy sat down on the edge of the bed. Jack winced, and she stood up quickly. "You're still hurting, aren't you?"

"A little," Jack said. "But I don't mind. Doc says he thinks the infection's gone and I can keep my leg."

"That's great news!" Sissy said.

"But he's still worried about a concussion."

Sissy shivered, and not just because of that news. The house was cold, and she thought maybe she and Peter ought to collect coal later on. But one bucket of coal wasn't going to help Jack. A whole wagonload wouldn't do that.

"I came to take Pete to see Willie Gilpin. So I can't stay now, but I'll come back to visit when I can," Sissy said. She nodded at Jack's brother, and the two started for the door.

"Sissy," Jack said in a low voice.

Sissy stopped.

"Ma's taking in laundry. She's paying Pa's gambling debt that way. She wants me to go back to school. Do you think if I study hard, I can catch up with the rest of the class? After all, I'm never going back to being a miner."

Sissy grinned. "You bet, Jack."

When the two reached the Gilpin house, Sissy took Peter up to Willie's room. Sissy had brought Peter several times that fall when she knew Mrs. Gilpin wouldn't be at home.

"I brought my marbles." Peter grinned. "Including the Red Devil."

"I'm going to win it this time," Willie said. "I've been practicing." Sometimes Sissy played marbles with him. Willie still wasn't as good as Peter, but he was better than Sissy.

Now Willie and Peter put their marbles in a circle on the floor. They took out their shooters. "You can go first," Willie said.

Peter polished his shooter on his chest. He knelt on the floor and shot. The marbles scattered. One went flying across the room, and Sissy crawled under the bed to retrieve it.

"Good shot," Willie said. He sat on the floor, leaning forward. He shot into the marbles that were left in the circle. The Red Devil flew out. Willie grinned. "Mine!" he said.

"Not for long," Peter told him.

The two continued the game, their voices rising as they won and lost marbles. "Got it back!" Peter yelled when the Red Devil changed hands again. Sissy didn't pay attention to how loud they were getting. She was concentrating on the game.

Suddenly, the door flew open. Startled, the three children looked up. Sissy expected to see Mrs. Ogden. Instead, Emma stood in the doorway. Sissy didn't know she was working that day. Her mouth dropped open.

"What's going on here?" Emma demanded. She put her hands on her hips.

"None of your business," Willie told her.

"Well, I guess it's your mother's business, you little brat."

"I'm going to tell her you called me that."

"And I'm going to tell her Sissy let that dirty Burke boy in here."

"Hey, I'm not dirty!" Peter said.

Sissy stood up and faced Emma. "There's no harm in Pete coming to visit."

Emma sniffed. "I know precious well you wouldn't bring him here if Mrs. Gilpin was around."

Sissy didn't answer.

Emma said, "That's what I thought."

Mrs. Ogden came into the room. "Oh my," she said when she saw Emma.

"She sneaked that awful Peter Burke in here."

Mrs. Ogden looked at the two boys with their marbles. "I guess there's no harm in that, Emma. They're having a good time."

"No harm!" Emma's voice was shrill. Sissy could see the

girl was enjoying herself. "I bet Mrs. Gilpin won't say that when I tell her."

"And why would you do that? Why would you tattle about something that makes Master William happy?" Mrs. Ogden asked.

Emma pursed her lips. "Because Mrs. Gilpin doesn't allow it, that's why. She told me herself that she doesn't want Master William's friends in the house. She said it would just upset him. She doesn't allow Master William to play with the boys from Chicken Flats. They're rough. He might get hurt."

"It doesn't upset me," Willie said. "Pete isn't going to hurt me."

"Yeah," Peter added. "It just upsets *you*. And what's wrong with boys from Chicken Flats? You live there, too."

Emma ignored the question and instead spoke to Willie. "It's not good for you. That's what the doctor said. I know."

"Watch it, girl. The rest of us know things, too. We know Master William is much better off when he has a friend to play with," Mrs. Ogden said. She put her hands on her hips, too, and glared at Emma.

"Yeah, you're not the boss here, Emma," Peter said.

"If you tell Mother, I'll call you a liar." Willie threatened.

Emma paused, thinking that over. "Do you expect Sissy and Mrs. Ogden to lie, too? What if your mother asks them? Are *they* going to say that boy wasn't here?"

"I'll tell Mother you're mean, and I don't want you to work for us anymore," Willie said.

"Now, Master William, that wouldn't be fair to Emma. You're too nice a boy to do that," Mrs. Ogden told him.

Everyone was quiet for a minute. Peter aimed his shooter at the marbles that were left. They scattered, and he had to get up to retrieve several from under the dresser. Then he sat down next to Willie.

"What do you want, Emma?" Sissy asked at last.

Emma looked at her, surprised. It was clear she wanted to make trouble. But she was starting to realize there might be something in it for her if she stayed quiet. She stared out the window before replying. "I think I ought to get paid more. After all, I do the work while Sissy sits here all day."

"Sissy does a great deal of work," said Mrs. Ogden. "Besides, you know I'm not in charge of wages."

Emma looked around the room. Watching her, Sissy wondered if Emma might ask for one of Willie's toys. Then

Emma gave Sissy a smile that was more of a sneer. "I know. Every time she comes here, Sissy has to clean the ashes out of the fireplaces."

"That's not possible. Mrs. Gilpin wouldn't allow it. Sissy is the tutor, and Mrs. Gilpin has given strict orders about her duties," Mrs. Ogden said.

Emma frowned, thinking hard.

"I'll give you my dessert for a week," Willie said.

"No, you'd just tell Cook to send up two desserts," Emma replied.

"But you'd still get one," Peter told her. He tossed his red marble from hand to hand.

Emma stared at it for a minute, then raised her chin. "I want your Red Devil."

Willie gasped. "That's not fair. It's Pete's."

Emma smirked. "Tough luck." She crossed her arms.

"You're not that mean, Emma," Sissy said. "I know things are tough, but you don't have to take it out on Pete."

"What do you know?" Emma snarled. "You have an easy job as a tutor because you're the doctor's daughter. You never have to worry. You don't know what it's like to have nothing to look forward to. You might even get away from Tenmile someday. But I'll never leave, and I'll never be anything more than somebody's hired girl."

"I'm sorry, Emma," Sissy said. She was just now realizing Emma was jealous of her. That was why she hated her.

Emma glanced at Mrs. Ogden. "I could tell Mrs. Gilpin you know all about Peter being here, Mrs. Ogden."

The housekeeper looked away. Sissy knew Mrs. Ogden needed her job as much as Emma needed hers. Was Emma really mean enough to tattle to Mrs. Gilpin?

Peter blew on the red marble and polished it against his shirt. Then he held it out. When Emma reached for it, he snatched it back. "If I give it to you, then you have to promise you'll never tell that I'm here. I'm coming back whenever Willie's mother is away."

Emma thought that over. "Okay."

"Cross your heart."

Emma made a cross on her chest. "Give me the marble now."

Willie shook his head. "Don't do it. We'll think of something else."

"It's all right. I'd rather come see you than have that old marble." Peter held out the Red Devil.

This time, Emma grabbed it. She rolled it around in her hand, then put it into her apron pocket. There was a look of triumph on her face. The others just stared at her. Sissy wondered if the marble was really that important to her. *No, it isn't the marble that matters to Emma. What matters is that Emma won. She's probably never won anything in her whole life.*

For a moment, Sissy felt sorry for her. Emma thought her life was so awful that she got pleasure from taking a little boy's prized possession. She felt even more sorry for Peter. But she also admired the boy. He'd given away his best marble to keep his friendship with Willie.

"I'm sorry," Sissy said after Mrs. Ogden said she and Emma had to get back to work.

"Me too," Willie said.

"It's worth it," Peter told them. Then he added, "I don't mind. You'd have won it off me anyway, Willie."

On her way home, Sissy stopped at the mercantile. "I want to buy a marble," she told the clerk.

"Just one?"

"Your very best one."

The clerk took out a sack of marbles and spread them on a tray. Most of the marbles were swirled, but there were several that were all one color. "Those are the best," he said. He went through the marbles, then held up one that was pale green with a rooster inside. "I'd pick that one. It's more expensive, but it's special."

"I don't care," Sissy said. She reached into her pocket and took out a coin. "It's for a special boy."

21

It was October now. Sissy was sure Nelle would never return to school. She had stopped to see her friend at the Ridge house several times since their last mushrooming trip, but Nelle was never home anymore, and Sissy didn't want to visit her at Delmonico's because of Mr. Ridge. One afternoon, she saw Essie leaving school and asked, "How is your sister?"

"She's busy at the restaurant," Essie replied. "She works there all the time now."

"I guess your dad made her quit school."

Essie nodded. "He says maybe next year I'll have to quit

school, too." It was cold, and Essie put her hands into the pockets of her frayed coat. She had a sad look on her face.

"Do you want to?"

"I gotta go," Essie said. Sissy watched the girl run off toward Chicken Flats.

That night at supper, Sissy told Doc and Greenie, "Nelle really did quit school, and Essie might have to, too. She told me so."

"Those poor girls," Greenie said.

"Can't we do anything for them?" Sissy asked.

Doc put down his fork. "Sissy, life isn't fair. We try our best, but we can't save everybody."

Sissy looked at Greenie, who was staring into her plate.

The next afternoon, Sissy stopped by the restaurant. When Nelle spotted her friend, she glanced toward her father, who was slicing ham. She gave Sissy a warning look. "I can't talk now," she said.

"Maybe Papa and I can come here for dinner tonight. I want to talk to you," Sissy whispered.

Nelle nodded. "I'd like that."

But when Sissy arrived home, Doc was hitching up the buggy. "Mrs. Burke sent for me. Jack has taken a bad turn," he told her. "You'd better come along."

"I thought he was doing better," Sissy said as she and Doc bounced over the road in the buggy.

"His leg is better, but his head is worse. That rockfall caused a pretty bad brain injury. When I saw Jack earlier this week, he complained of terrible headaches. He'd been vomiting, and he was mumbling nonsense. And he couldn't seem to stay awake."

"I haven't seen him for a week. I should have stopped by sooner."

"You've done a great deal for him. Your visits kept up his spirits. They were better for that boy than anything I could've done," Doc told her. He never praised Sissy unless he meant it, and the compliment warmed her.

"Nothing's going to do any good, though, is it?" Sissy held her breath, hoping Doc would say she was wrong.

"I don't know."

"Oh, Papa, can't you do something?"

Doc shook his head. "I examined him two days ago.

Based on what I saw then, I don't think anybody can. I believe the brain injury is fatal. The boy doesn't have long to live."

Sissy put her arms around herself and squeezed tight. "Oh, Papa."

"I can't heal everyone. I wish I could, Sis, but I'm not God." He paused. "I know how much Jack means to you, but you have to be strong for him and for his family, too. Some people think prayer works. Maybe it does. You might try that."

Sissy bowed her head, but like Papa, she wasn't sure prayer was the answer. She'd already prayed for Jack.

When Doc and Sissy arrived, Jack told them, "I don't know why I'm hanging on. I'm no good to anybody." His voice was slurred, and it took him a long time to get the words out.

"Don't give up," Sissy insisted.

Doc examined Jack, then shook his head. "You stay with him," he told Sissy. "I have another patient I have to see. I'll be back as soon as I can."

Sissy sat down in a chair beside Jack. "I'll read to you," she said. Willie always loved it when she read to him. Maybe Jack would, too. But he had dropped off to sleep and didn't hear her.

Sissy went into the kitchen, where Mrs. Burke stood beside baby Nancy's cradle, wringing her hands in her apron.

"Jack can't stay awake. He's so weak. He wouldn't eat his breakfast or his dinner. I'm afraid . . ." Her face was gray, her eyes red from crying.

"I'll take care of Nancy. You go lie down," Sissy said. Mrs. Burke started to protest, but Sissy insisted. She picked up the baby, who had begun to fuss. "Go," she told Mrs. Burke, who went into the bedroom and closed the door.

Sissy played with Nancy for a long time. She sang to her and made faces and held her up so she could stretch her legs. When Nancy laughed, Sissy took her to the bed so Jack could see her, thinking she might cheer him up. But Jack was still asleep. The baby, too, was getting sleepy, and Sissy returned her to the cradle. She was tidying the front room when Doc returned.

"How is he?" Doc asked.

Sissy shrugged. "I don't know. I've been checking him

every few minutes, but he's still sleeping." She took a deep breath. "Papa, I can barely hear him breathe."

Doc sat down beside Jack and was examining him when Mrs. Burke came out of the bedroom. "I heard voices. I thought Jack . . ." She trailed off when she saw it was Doc she'd heard.

Doc rose and took Mrs. Burke's hands. "We've done everything we can for him. It won't be long now. I'm sorry."

Sissy brought two more chairs, and the three sat down beside the bed. Evening came on, and Mr. Burke returned from his shift. Jack's brothers arrived home from school. Sissy quietly explained that Jack didn't have long to live, and the two boys held on to each other as they cried. Then they were all quiet, listening hard for Jack's breath. Finally, Jack gasped and the breathing stopped.

Doc stood and listened to Jack's heart with a stethoscope. He shook his head. "I'm sorry." He pulled the blanket up to Jack's chin.

Both Mr. and Mrs. Burke began crying. Peter and Little Joe did, too. They clutched each other. When the baby started to fuss, Mrs. Burke went into the kitchen to tend to her. Little Joe hit the wall with his fists, and Mr. Burke picked him up and held him close. Peter stayed by the bed.

"How come he had to die, Papa?" Sissy asked. Her voice broke. "How come he couldn't live longer?"

Doc shook his head. "I don't know, Sis. I wish I could have saved him, but I couldn't. It's not easy to accept. I'm sorry to leave, but another patient needs me. I'll see you at home." Doc gave Sissy a rare hug, then gripped Mrs. Burke's arm and shook Mr. Burke's hand before he left.

Mr. Burke took Little Joe outside, where a group of boys was waiting. Through the open doorway, Sissy could see them. In a mining town, people always sensed when something was wrong. The boys kicked at the dirt and glanced sideways at each other.

"I'm sorry, boys," Mr. Burke said. "Jackie went to sleep tonight. Our boy is gone forever."

Sissy and Peter stood alone beside Jack's body. Sissy reached out and took Peter's hand. Tears ran down the faces of the two children. Peter rubbed his eyes, trying to stop his tears.

"Jack would understand if you cried," Sissy said.

Peter turned and put his wet face against Sissy. He cried for a long time. Then he reached down and touched Jack's forehead with his fingers. He straightened up and saluted.

"Tap 'er light, Jack."

It was dark when Sissy got home, but instead of going into the house, she headed up the mountain to her special place. The squirrel ran down the tree and stared at her.

"He's dead," Sissy told the little animal. "Jack wanted to leave Tenmile, but not like this. I hate this town. It killed Jack, and it's spoiled Nelle's life."

Sissy banged her fists against an aspen trunk until they hurt. She sat down in a pile of dead leaves and cried. She finally stopped when she realized Greenie would worry if she didn't come home soon. Sissy rose and slowly walked down the slope until she could see out over the town.

"I hate you, Tenmile!" she yelled. "I hate you!"

22

CHRISTMAS WAS BEAUTIFUL ON THE Tenmile Range. It had been snowing since October, but the howling blizzards that swept down the mountainsides and sent biting cold through the thin walls of the shacks in Chicken Flats hadn't yet arrived. Instead, snow fell in huge fluffy flakes. Sissy wished Jack could've seen them. He'd loved the snow. But he'd been gone nearly two months.

"The flakes are big enough to catch on your tongue," Sissy said as she and Peter walked through the falling snow. They'd taken Little Joe sledding on the mine dump after school. Sissy reached over with her mittened hand and brushed snow off Peter's check. "If you stay still very long, you'll turn into a snowman."

The flakes floated down and covered the mine dumps and ore piles. They made the ground seem as pure as the forest. The roads had a coating of ice just thick enough that Peter and Little Joe could "skate" on them in their rough shoes on their way to school. Sissy had seen older boys grab on to the backs of ore wagons and slide along behind them. While that might be fun, it was dangerous. Sissy remembered Toby, the boy whose legs had been broken when he was run over by an ore wagon last summer. She was glad that none of the boys had been hurt since the snow had started.

When the snow stopped falling, the sun came out. The roofs of the shacks seemed to smoke as the snow steamed off them. Sunlight bounced off ice crystals and thin crusts of snow, making them shimmer. Sissy had seen men working outdoors with half circles of charcoal under their eyes to keep from going snow-blind.

"I would do that, too," Sissy told Peter, "but I'd look like a raccoon."

As they walked through town, the three stopped to look in store windows filled with Christmas toys. Little Joe studied the bright red sleds and wagons, the skates and stuffed bears. China dolls resting in toy buggies stared back at him with unblinking eyes the clear blue color of columbine flowers. There were sets of jacks and marbles and toy dishes. Candy canes hung on strings stretched across the windows. Sissy knew that children from Chicken Flats like Little Joe would never be able to play with such toys or taste treats like those, but they could dream.

"One day, I'm going to have a jackknife like that, one with two blades," Little Joe told Sissy. The boy's face was pressed so hard against the store window that his nose left a smudge when he stepped back. "And I'm going to buy Nancy that dolly." He pointed to the biggest doll in the display. It had real hair and eyes that opened and shut.

"Who can afford to buy those things?" Sissy asked Greenie when she returned home. She knew her family was better off than many people in Tenmile. But even Sissy had never had a doll two feet tall with hair the color of a ten-dollar gold piece.

"Maybe some of those toys are just for display and they'll be stored away until next Christmas," Greenie replied. "But you're right—the children in Chicken Flats certainly won't find them under the Christmas tree. They'll be lucky to get a doll made from a stocking or a 'baseball' made from a piece of leather with yarn wrapped around it."

If they were truly fortunate, Chicken Flats children like the Burke boys would discover oranges and handfuls of nuts in their stockings, too. They would devour the oranges, or maybe try to make them last as long as possible by eating only a segment each hour. The peels would go to their mothers to flavor pudding and cookies.

The schools held their own holiday celebrations. A banner with "Happy Christmas" was stretched across the front of Sissy's classroom. Children drew chalk stars on the blackboard. They staged a Christmas pageant, voting on who got to play Mary and Joseph.

Sissy remembered how Jack had been chosen to play Joseph the year before. She blinked back tears as she recalled how proud he had been at the honor. Sissy hadn't been chosen to play Mary.

"Maybe you didn't get it because the kids are jealous that you're so ambitious for a girl, since you want to go to college." He laughed. "After all, Mary didn't go to college."

"Maybe she wanted to," Sissy had replied.

A week before Christmas, Willie asked Sissy to select a Christmas present for Peter. "I'd ask Mother, but she doesn't know I'm seeing Pete. I want to give him something special. I was thinking maybe skates."

For weeks, the ponds around Tenmile had been frozen solid, and Willie had seen skaters from his bedroom window. "What do you think?" he asked.

Sissy thought skates would be a wonderful gift. Few boys in Chicken Flats had real ice skates. They made their own out of scraps of metal or slid on the ice in their shoes. But skates were a luxury. Peter needed something practical.

Sissy shook her head. "Boots," she said.

"Boots? You mean everyday boots?"

Sissy nodded.

"That's no fun. Who wants to open a present and find boots?"

"Peter Burke does. He needs them. Haven't you noticed? The soles of his boots are worn out. He has to put cardboard inside to keep his feet warm. Then the cardboard gets wet. The toes are almost worn through, too."

"His mother ought to buy him new ones."

Sissy stared at Willie. Did he really think people in Chicken Flats could buy boots whenever they needed them? "She can't afford them."

Willie looked away, frowning. Then he said, "I've never been to Pete's house. Are they poor?"

Sissy didn't know how to answer. Some of the families who lived in Chicken Flats were indeed poor. They didn't have warm clothes or enough to eat. The Burkes weren't much better off, but they never complained or felt sorry for themselves.

"No, they're not poor," Sissy said slowly. "They just don't have any money."

That night at supper, Greenie said, "I was at the grocer's today. Someone told me that the Ridge girls are gone. Been gone a week."

"Nelle and Essie?" Sissy asked.

"That's what I heard."

"Gone where?" Sissy asked. Had things gotten so bad

with their father that they'd run away after all? She hadn't seen Nelle since shortly after Jack had been buried.

"It's said that they went to live with an aunt in Denver."

Sissy shook her head. "They don't have an aunt. Nelle told me they don't have any relatives at all."

"Hmm," Greenie said.

When Greenie wouldn't look at her, Sissy asked, "Did you have something to do with this?"

"With what?" Greenie asked. She raised her coffee cup to her mouth to hide a smile.

"With Nelle and Essie leaving."

Doc looked up from his supper plate. "Yes, do you know anything about this, Mrs. Greenway?"

Greenie wiped her mouth with her napkin. She set the napkin on the table. "Well, if I had to, I might be able to guess what happened. I might guess that somebody's housekeeper has a friend in Denver who'd lost her son and was awful lonely for children in her big house. That friend might have wanted to take in two sweet little girls. They could go to school during the week and help her with her housework on the weekends. An awful nice lady like that would love those girls and be a mother to them."

Sissy didn't understand. "Nelle said her father would never let them go. What happened?"

"Let's just say that housekeeper knew all about how Mr. Ridge treated those girls. She might have threatened to tell people. Think of what that would have done to business at Delmonico's. She might even have said she'd tell the newspaper."

"The newspaper?" Doc asked. "Would they really have printed anything?"

Greenie shrugged. "Maybe I told Mr. Ridge *you'd* tell the newspaper, Doc. They would have believed *you*."

Doc thought that over, then nodded. "I don't like to interfere in my patients' personal business, but maybe I should have this time. You were braver than I was, Mrs. Greenway. You did the right thing."

When supper was over and the dishes were washed and put away, Sissy put on her coat and boots and stepped outside. It was too cold and snowy to go all the way up to her special place, so she sat on the back porch steps. She looked up at the sky. There were millions of stars, the same stars she and Jack used to look at together. Now Jack was up there somewhere, looking down on her—and on Nelle.

Sissy hugged herself. Perhaps Nelle was looking up at the stars, too. Even better, maybe Nelle was inside by a warm fire with Essie, the two of them doing their homework. Sissy hoped so. And she hoped that wherever Nelle was, she was thinking of Jack and her, too.

23

ALTHOUGH CHRISTMAS BROUGHT JOY, it could be a cruel time for Tenmile's poor. Sissy knew that many families didn't have money for presents. Greenie had told her about men who went into the saloons and drank up the cash intended for gifts. Many children hung up stockings and found them still empty in the morning. They had no ornaments or Christmas trees. Worst of all, Sissy thought, there was no Christmas dinner.

The church women helped those poor families as much as they could. Everyone pitched in. "We can at least keep Old Man Sorrow away for a day or two," Greenie told Sissy as she sat at the kitchen table finishing a pair of stockings for a Christmas basket.

She knitted stockings for the poor all year long and made flannel baby blankets and caps that went into the charity baskets. Sissy regularly gave clothes she had outgrown and toys she no longer played with to their church. Doc dropped coins into jars set up in stores and saloons. The merchants gave items they couldn't sell. All the donations were brought to a meeting hall a few days before Christmas, and the women from the churches in Tenmile gathered to fill gift baskets for the neediest families in Chicken Flats.

As the owner of the largest mine on the Tenmile, Mr. Gilpin gave two hundred dollars every year to the charity effort. The women used all the monies donated to purchase hams and chickens, sugar and flour, coffee and tea. Sissy helped Greenie fill the baskets. The women would deliver them the next day to the families on a list the churches put together. Sissy had never helped deliver the baskets before.

"Some of your school friends will get these baskets. I think you're grown-up enough now not to show you're shocked when you see how poor they are," Greenie said.

As she was putting a flannel blanket into a basket, Sissy

looked up to see Mr. Gilpin. He had come by the meeting hall to drop off Willie's outgrown clothes.

"Why, happy Christmas, Sissy," Mr. Gilpin said. "Now I know why Willie was complaining that you didn't come to see him today."

"I can't. I'm helping with the baskets. They're for families in Chicken Flats." She wondered if Mr. Gilpin knew that some of the fathers and brothers in those families worked at the Yellowcat. She introduced Greenie.

"I hope you don't mind that Sissy isn't able to work with your son today," Greenie said. "We need her here."

"I'm sure Mrs. Gilpin understands," he said.

Sissy wasn't so sure.

"Sissy always seems to be around when someone needs help," Mr. Gilpin said.

Sissy blushed as Greenie replied, "She is a remarkable girl."

"Yes, she is."

The next morning, Sissy, Greenie, and Greenie's friend Mrs.

Mrs. East began delivering the baskets. "It's a wonderful feeling knowing you've helped people, if only a little bit," Greenie said.

Greenie was right. At each house, they were welcomed by families who were excited and thankful. Sissy felt good knowing that she, too, was helping people at Christmas. But she also felt guilty when she compared her nice house to the shacks in Chicken Flats. She saw how many people were ill and that the women were overworked and the children undernourished. A few of the men were home, bedridden with the "miner's puff"—tuberculosis—from working in the damp conditions of the mine. Sissy wished she could tell them to visit Doc, that he wouldn't charge if they couldn't pay, but she knew they were too proud.

Several families seemed reluctant to accept the baskets, but Greenie seemed to know that and had a way of putting people at ease. She didn't make the Christmas baskets appear to be charity. They stopped at a house in the Mexican section of Chicken Flats. When a woman opened the door, Sissy caught the scent of fiery red chili peppers cooking on the stove. The woman looked embarrassed when she saw the basket.

Greenie told her, "It's Christmas, a time to share. It would please us if you would accept, Mrs. Gonzales." Then she frowned a little and added, "It would be a kindness if you were not too critical of my fruitcake. It did not turn out well this year."

"Oh, I'm sure it's just fine," Mrs. Gonzales replied.

Greenie and Mrs. East and Sissy didn't linger, just called "Happy Christmas!" and went on to a section of Chicken Flats called Swedetown. Sissy knew from a friend that the traditional Swedish Christmas dinner was rice porridge and fish that had been soaked in lye water for six days. But when Sissy peered through the open door of the next house, she saw that the stove was cold and there was no sign of Christmas dinner. The woman who had answered put her hands together in a prayerful gesture, thanking the women for the basket. Her children gathered around and peered inside, exclaiming over the treats.

"We have to hurry and finish up before shift change," Mrs. East said after they left the Swedish woman's house.

"How come?" Sissy asked.

"The working men won't like to be seen taking charity," she explained.

Sissy could tell that the women were embarrassed, too, but they had no choice but to take the baskets. She understood that they were the ones who wept into their aprons when there were no presents for the children on Christmas morning. A man might grumble and refuse a basket, but even if she was reluctant, a woman always accepted with gratitude. She knew that without the basket, her children would have little or nothing for Christmas.

Some women insisted that Greenie, Mrs. East, and Sissy come in. An Italian woman asked them to taste her panettone, a sweet bread studded with dried cherries and pine nuts. Another woman even offered them sweet wine, which they graciously declined.

"I'll just heat up the coffee," a woman said when they stopped at a house with Christmas stars pasted to the window. "The grounds ain't been used but once before." The three didn't want to give the impression that they were too good to stop and visit, so they went inside.

Drinking the coffee, Greenie said, "It's as good as I ever tasted." Sissy knew Greenie was fibbing because the coffee was the color of black ink. And it tasted like black ink, too.

"I wish we could do more," Mrs. East said after they left

a house where a Scottish woman had offered a slice of the shortbread she'd made for Christmas. "They need so much."

Greenie nodded. "Our food baskets, like the angels' visits, are few and far between."

Delivering the baskets was rewarding for Sissy. She loved the way the children gathered around to peer inside. She loved seeing their eyes light up. But she was shocked by how poor and needy the families were. Some of the people were sick, and several of the women were widows with small children. Many of the houses were no more than cold and drafty shacks.

By the time the three had delivered all but one basket, Sissy was tired from tramping through the snow on such a cold day. She didn't pay attention to the last house. Most of the dwellings on Chicken Flats looked the same to her. This one was a little shabbier than the others, however. There was no sign of Christmas decorations in the window. Sissy stood behind Greenie as the woman knocked on the door. When it opened, Greenie said, "Happy Christmas, Emma."

Sissy looked up quickly. *Emma?* Sissy was shocked to see her. She watched Emma's eyes light up as she saw the Christmas basket. Sissy tried to turn away so Emma wouldn't notice her, but it was too late. As Emma reached out to take the basket, she spotted Sissy. Her eyes grew cold. She pulled her hand back. "What's this?" she asked.

"Just something for the little ones at Christmas," Greenie said. "Treats we wanted to share and some stockings I knitted." Greenie smiled. "I hope you'll overlook the knots. I suspect you're much better at knitting than I am. And I think there are jacks and a doll tucked in there, too. We just stopped by to wish you a happy Christmas."

A little girl came to stand beside Emma. Although there was snow on the ground, the girl was barefoot. Sissy looked through the door and caught a glimpse of a woman lying on a bed. Emma's father was dead, and now it looked like her mother was bedridden. Maybe she'd gotten the miner's puff from her husband.

Greenie saw the woman, too. "Bring your mother to see Doc Carlson. Maybe he can give her something to ease her troubles." Greenie pushed the basket toward Emma.

Emma looked down at her little sister before glancing

back at her mother. She turned to Greenie, straightened her shoulders, and stared at the basket.

Then looking directly at Sissy, Emma said, "We thank you, but we don't need your charity. Give the basket to someone who does." She firmly shut the door.

"I don't understand. From what I've heard, that family needs help more than anybody. They don't have a thing," Mrs. East said.

Sissy stared at the closed door for a long time. Had Emma turned down the basket because of her? She hoped not, because Mrs. East was right. Emma's family was poor, and they needed help. But Sissy understood. She knew Emma had one thing—her pride.

24

"Why would a mother want her son to stay in the house all the time and not go outside and play?" Sissy asked Doc one evening in January.

"Are you talking about the Gilpin boy?" Doc asked.

"I was just wondering."

"I've told you, Sis—you are not to interfere."

"I think he would be all right if he just got outside in the fresh air."

"That's up to his mother. You're not a doctor."

"But Papa, don't you think I *could* be a doctor? I'd like to make people better the way you do." Sissy had been thinking more and more about that ever since Jack had died.

Doc laughed. "Girls can't be doctors."

"Why not?"

"Because they're girls. You could think about being a nurse."

"I don't want to be a nurse. I want to be a doctor. Greenie told me there's a medical school in Boulder that takes women."

Doc looked up and glared at Greenie, who turned her eyes to her knitting. He picked up his book. "If you were a doctor, you'd know not to interfere. Leave the Gilpin boy alone."

Sissy didn't want to go against her father's wishes, but when a sunny day in January came along, she thought it wouldn't hurt to let Willie escape the house for a few minutes.

Peter had come to visit that morning, wearing the boots Willie had given him for Christmas. "They're great for skating on the street," he said. "The ice is perfect. I wish we could go outside together and skate."

"Me too," Willie said. Then he looked up at Sissy. "Why can't we?"

Sissy didn't see any harm in it. And Mrs. Gilpin wouldn't know, since she was away for the day visiting a friend. "I'll think about it," she said. "But you have to finish your spelling lesson first."

"I'll help," Peter said.

"How do you spell 'skate'?" Sissy asked.

"Um . . . ?" Peter said.

"I know. S-K-A-T-E. Lesson done," Willie said. "Now can I go outside, Sissy? Please? I haven't been out in the snow for such a long time. I love the snow."

Sissy heard the pleading in the boy's voice and took a deep breath. Although she'd been thinking about it, she knew letting Willie go outside was a big decision. What if Mrs. Gilpin found out? She'd be so angry. Sissy looked again at Willie, whose eyes were shining at the thought of playing in the snow.

"I guess it wouldn't hurt," she said.

"Yay!" the two boys shouted together.

Willie laced up heavy boots. Then Sissy wrapped him in a warm coat and muffler while Peter put on his own coat.

With Sissy following behind, the two boys clumped down the front stairs. Just then, Mrs. Ogden came out of the kitchen.

"What in the world?"

"The boys are going to play in the snow," Sissy said.

"Does Mrs. Gilpin know?"

Sissy shook her head.

"Well, you'd better come back in before she's home." Mrs. Ogden smiled. "I'll have hot chocolate waiting."

Peter grinned. "Come on, Willie."

The two boys rushed outside so fast Sissy could barely keep up with them. The three started to skate on the icy road. Willie couldn't keep his balance and fell.

"Uh-oh," Sissy said.

She rushed over to the boy to help him up, but Willie was already on his feet, and he grinned at her. "It didn't hurt."

The two boys chased each other back and forth across the icy street, playing tag. Peter fell, and Willie cried, "I won!"

"Like heck!" As Peter got to his knees, he made a snowball and threw it at Willie.

"Hey, no fair!" Willie yelled. He pushed Peter's face into the snow. Soon, the two were tossing snowballs back and forth. They stopped when Willie threw a snowball that hit Sissy on the cheek. "Gee, I'm sorry," Willie said.

Sissy frowned at him. Then she made a snowball. She threw it at Willie. It hit him in the chest.

"It's war!" Peter called as he bombarded his friends with snowballs. The fight lasted until Willie fell over, exhausted.

Arm in arm, the boys went through the front door and up the stairs to Willie's room. Sissy went into the kitchen for the hot chocolate.

"Is he dead?" Mrs. Ogden asked, smiling.

"He's just fine."

"Good. I was afraid—"

"Me too."

"I'm glad he went outside. It's good for him." Mrs. Ogden handed the tray with three cups of hot chocolate on it to Sissy.

The two boys were so loud, joking and laughing as they drank their hot chocolate, that they didn't hear the bedroom door open. Emma stuck her head inside the room. Sissy was startled; she hadn't realized Emma was working that day.

"What's going on?" Emma asked. She stared at Willie, his face red, his hair still wet from the snow. "You went outside!"

"That's not any of your business," Sissy said.

"It is, too. He's not supposed to do that. I'm going to tell." Before Sissy could stop her, Emma yelled, "Mrs. Gilpin, come quick! Look what Sissy did." Emma took the Red Devil from her apron pocket and tossed it from hand to hand, taunting the boys.

Sissy was horrified. When had the Gilpins returned? She hadn't noticed them come in. She was in for it now. What was worse, so was Willie. He looked frightened as his mother rushed into the room.

"What's going on here?" Mrs. Gilpin asked. "Who is that? Is that Peter Burke? What's he doing here?"

Peter slunk into a corner of the bedroom.

"He came to play with me," Willie said.

"Who gave him permission?"

"I did," Sissy admitted softly.

"They were playing outside in the snow," Emma said.

Mrs. Gilpin's mouth dropped open. "What!"

"It's all right, Mother. We had a snowball fight. It was fun."

"Are you hurt?"

"Of course not."

"You could have been!"

Mr. Gilpin came into the room. "But he wasn't, Mother. Look at him. He looks just fine. And healthy. Maybe it's time Willie is allowed to act like a normal boy again. Being outside is good for him. Look how happy he is."

"I don't know, Father. I'd worry if I knew he was outdoors roughhousing in the snow or playing on the mine dumps."

"And I'd worry more if Willie never got a chance to enjoy life."

Mrs. Gilpin was silent for a few seconds. "Is that what you want, William?"

"More than anything!"

Mrs. Gilpin tapped her toe as she thought. "Maybe we could give it a try. But I want you to be careful. And I want Sissy to go with you when you play outside."

Willie and Peter looked at each other and grinned.

Mr. Gilpin put his hand on Willie's back. "Maybe in time you would like to go down in the hole again."

"Yes, sir!" Willie yelled. "Can Pete come, too?"

"I wouldn't have it any other way."

Sissy, wanting to give the Gilpins some privacy, started to leave the room. Mr. Gilpin stopped her.

"Was it your idea to bring Peter here? I've noticed Willie has seemed stronger and happier since you started working with him."

Sissy's face turned red, and she looked away. "Yes . . ."

She glanced at Emma, who was scowling. Things hadn't turned out the way Emma had hoped. Emma could have ruined everything for Willie—and for Sissy, too. Then Sissy remembered the Christmas basket Emma had turned down and her sick mother. No wonder she was unhappy.

"Mine . . . and Emma's."

Emma's head jerked up. She studied Sissy for a moment, perhaps waiting to see if Sissy would add something to get her in trouble. When Sissy didn't say anything more, Emma nodded at her. Sissy nodded back.

"They say young Willie Gilpin is playing outside again. I heard he even visited the mine with his father," Doc said a few weeks later. He and Sissy were in the surgery. Sissy was washing instruments.

She stared at the basin of water. *Now I'll get it*, she

thought, and didn't answer.

"Is that right?"

"Yes, sir."

"Are you responsible?"

"Sort of." Sissy glanced at Doc, then looked away again. She couldn't tell how angry he was.

"I thought so. Mr. Gilpin came by yesterday to thank me."

"I know you said I shouldn't—"

Doc held up his hand. "No, you shouldn't have. Something could have happened to that boy."

"But it didn't."

"No, it didn't."

25

By the time April arrived, it seemed to Sissy that the snow would never stop. It came down in sheets of white. Greenie called spring storms "willow benders" because they were thick and heavy and wet. They bent trees and broke their branches. Throughout Tenmile, men shoveled snow off roofs to keep them from caving in. The wind blew drifts as high as the tops of windows.

Doc shivered as he sat at the kitchen table. He was eating breakfast and reading the newspaper by the light of a kerosene lamp; it was still early and dark outside. Sissy had her back to the cookstove to keep warm. She dreaded walking to school in the cold. She could hear the wind blowing outside.

Greenie picked up the coffeepot from the stove and poured coffee for Doc. Then she filled a cup for herself and sat down. "Are you going to continue as Willie's tutor now that he's started going to your school?"

"Willie's going to the Tenmile school? Did Mrs. Gilpin approve that?" Doc asked, looking over the top of his paper.

"At first, she wasn't sure. Willie told me *he* wanted to go. His father agreed," Sissy said. "Mrs. Gilpin arranged for Pete to look out for Willie at school. She thinks he needs someone with him all the time, though he really doesn't—Willie and Pete dreamed that up. She's paying Pete twenty-five cents a week."

"Oh, for goodness' sake, Willie won't walk all the way to school in weather like this, will he? That's a treacherous road. What if he slips?" Greenie asked.

"Somebody drives him in a carriage."

"Well, isn't that fine," Greenie said. "I'd hate to think of that poor boy wading through this snow all the way down the mountain from the Gilpin place. I hate to think of you walking to school in this weather, too, Sissy, but there's nothing to be done about it. You'd best be on your way."

Sissy sighed. It was pleasant beside the stove. She pulled on her boots and reached for her coat. Just then, she heard a sound outside. It came from the direction of the Yellowcat.

Doc looked up. "What was that?"

The three of them stopped and listened as a sharp whistle sounded. "It's not time for shift change," Greenie said.

"That's the signal for an accident," Doc said. "I better see if I can help."

"Isn't it time they hire a doctor to stay up at the mine?" Greenie asked.

Doc nodded. "They're talking about it. Mr. Gilpin asked me if I wanted the job, but I wasn't interested. It would take me away from my regular work. The townsfolk need me down here. But I better go on up to the Cat now and see what's happened."

Doc's heavy coat was hanging from a hook on the wall. He took it down and grabbed his sheepskin hat. As he reached for his thick gloves, he turned to Sissy. "Well, come on, then."

"You'll let me go with you?"

"I might need a nurse."

The two trudged up the hill to the Yellowcat, the sleety snow stinging their faces like broken glass. Doc didn't take the buggy because he didn't want the horse standing out in the cold. Besides, the road to the mine was steep and icy.

Other people had heard the mine whistle and were streaming out of the houses in Chicken Flats. Sissy recognized them as the families of the mine workers. Women, bundled up in layers of skirts and shawls, held babies or clutched the hands of small children as they hurried toward the Yellowcat. Many were immigrants and talked in languages Sissy didn't know, but she could understand the fear in their voices.

Sissy spotted Peter in the crowd and yelled his name. The boy stopped. "What's happened?" he asked.

Sissy shook her head. "I don't know, but I'm going with Doc to see if anyone's hurt."

"My pa's underground. I told Ma to stay home with Nancy while I checked on him."

"Oh, Pete! I hope he's all right."

A crowd had already gathered by the time Doc, Sissy, and Peter reached the mine. The guards were telling people to stand back. Doc pushed to the front of the crowd.

"I'm Doctor Carlson. This is my nurse."

"We're glad you're here, Doc," a guard said, stepping aside to let them pass. Peter slipped in with them. "There's been a cave-in. We think six or seven men are hurt. Maybe more. They're starting to bring them up now."

"Where can we put the injured? We can't treat them outdoors," Doc said. The wind was whipping the snow around so hard that Sissy could barely see the gallows frame, the superstructure over the mine.

"The office," the guard replied.

There was a commotion at the mine entrance as men carried two miners outside. Women pushed forward, shouting, calling the names of their husbands.

"Who is it?" one woman yelled.

"It's George, I know it's George," another cried.

Doc shoved his way past people milling around the mine, Sissy and Peter behind him. He quickly examined the two men. One appeared to have two broken legs. The other man had a bloody and mangled arm. Both had head wounds and were unconscious.

"Get a wagon over here, quick. And blankets," Doc said.

"We'll have to take them down to the surgery. I can't operate here."

"Don't you want to wait for the others?" a guard asked.

"I have to get started. It could be a while before you can bring them all up."

"Who's going to take care of the men here if you're gone?"

"My daughter will."

"This girl?"

"She's as good a nurse as we have on the Tenmile. Sissy, you stay here and tend to the men as they come up." He handed her his medical bag. "If their injuries aren't serious, you can treat them in the mine office and let them go home. Send anybody who's badly hurt to the surgery. Pete, you make sure nobody interferes with her. She's in charge here. Quick, now. There's no time to waste."

One of the guards fetched a wagon, and he and the driver carefully lifted the injured miners into the bed. Doc climbed in beside them.

"But Papa . . ." Sissy protested.

"You have to take charge. There's no one else to do it. If I stay here, these men could die."

Sissy stared at Doc as the wagon started down the hill.

I'm in charge? She shivered. *What if I do something wrong?* She was frightened, but she knew she didn't have time to be. Other miners were being helped out of the mine. She saw a wounded man look around, confused.

"Take him to the mine office," she told the two men with him. Her voice sounded weak. *Can I really do what Papa asks? I've never treated anybody on my own except for Mr. Washington, and he wasn't very sick. How can I take charge of all these miners?*

One of the men with the wounded miner stared at her. "Hey, where did the doc go? You're nothing but a little girl. What can you do?"

"Doctor Carlson left me in charge. You do what I tell you." Sissy's voice was stronger now.

"Yeah, Doc left her in charge," the guard repeated. "Do what she says."

Sissy and Peter followed the men into the office. They laid the miner on a cot. "I need hot water—lots of it. And more cots and blankets," she told one of the men. There was more authority in her voice now. She took a deep breath as she stared down at the miner. *I can do this,* she told herself. She washed the miner's face. *Thank goodness! The cuts aren't serious. I can treat them.*

"Did any of the falling rocks hit your head?" she asked the man.

"No, ma'am."

"You're lucky. You're going to be all right. Just sit here for a few minutes, and then you can leave." Sissy turned to Peter. "Get his name, then go outside and announce that he's fine."

A minute later, Sissy heard Peter yell the man's name. A woman quickly made her way through the crowd. "I'm his wife," she said. Peter let her through.

Another wounded miner was brought into the office. He was bleeding from a deep cut on his arm. *I can handle this one. There's no need to send him to Papa,* Sissy told herself.

"I'll clean your wound, then stitch it shut," she told the miner.

"You?" the man asked.

"Do you know any man who's better at sewing than a woman?" she retorted. The miner laughed. So did Sissy. She felt more confident now. "Maybe I could send you home and your wife could do it," she joked.

The next miner was more seriously wounded. His leg was so badly smashed that Sissy wondered if it would have to be amputated. She tried to stop the bleeding, but blood still came through the bandages. She told Peter to get another wagon. Fast. When the driver arrived, Sissy said, "You get this man to the surgery as quick as you can. Tell Doc Carlson I said he's a priority."

"Yes, ma'am." He and a guard loaded the man into the wagon. Then the driver took off, yelling, "Wounded man! Get out of the way!"

After a couple more men with mild wounds were treated, someone else limped into the office, supported by a fellow miner.

"Pa!" Peter shouted. "Are you okay, Pa? Sissy'll look after you." Peter rushed to his father and helped him sit down.

Mr. Burke grinned at Sissy. "You the doctor now? Well, I don't expect there's a better one on the Tenmile."

Sissy told him to take off his boot. "Your ankle's sprained," she said after she examined it. She wrapped it in bandages. "Don't walk on it any more than you have to," she told him. "Pete, get a wagon to drop off your pa at home."

"Should I go with him?"

Sissy thought that over. "No, I need you here. We still don't know if other men have been hurt," she said.

Peter puffed up with pride at her words. "Is that all right, Pa?"

"You stay and help Sissy," Mr. Burke told his son.

"This is the last of them," a guard told Sissy as another man came in. "Ten men total were hurt." Doc had taken two men with him, and Sissy had sent a third to the surgery. She had treated the rest herself.

As she examined the last miner, Mr. Gilpin came into the office. He was surprised to see her. "What are you doing here? Where is Doctor Carlson?"

Sissy was busy examining the patient's head and only glanced at Mr. Gilpin. "My father's in the surgery at home. I'm checking the injured here first. If anyone needs help I can't give, I'm sending them to him." She turned to Peter. "I think Doc ought to take a look at this man. He got hit on the head, and it looks serious. Find a wagon." She knew to be cautious. After all, Jack had died from a head injury.

"You're in charge here?" Mr. Gilpin asked.

"Yes, sir," Sissy told him.

"Look what she done to me, Mr. Gilpin," the miner with the gashed arm said. He held it up. "She sewed it shut. Pretty fancy stitching if you ask me."

Sissy nodded at him. "I think you're all right to go home now. Make sure you rest and come see Doc tomorrow." She helped the man stand.

"He can't walk through this snow," Mr. Gilpin said. He turned to one of the guards. "Make sure this man has a way home. In fact, organize a ride for anyone who needs one. And bring coffee and food for the others."

Sissy had been so busy with the last miner that she hadn't paid much attention to Mr. Gilpin. Now she realized he was staring at her. She wondered if he was angry. He clearly hadn't expected a girl to be tending to his employees. She stood up straight, trying to appear taller.

Mr. Gilpin frowned at her. "Do you know what you're doing?"

"Yes, sir. I've worked with my father for years, and he trusts me."

Mr. Gilpin nodded. "When you're finished, you and Peter go to our house and tell Mrs. Ogden to give you something warm to eat," Mr. Gilpin said. "I'd take you myself, but I want to visit with the injured men."

Sissy shook her head. "I can't, sir. I have to go to the surgery to help Doc now that we've seen all the injured men here."

"I understand." Mr. Gilpin stared at her for a moment. Then he told the guard, "Get her a ride to the doctor's house. And take this boy home."

Sissy thanked him. She was tired and wasn't looking forward to the long walk back through the snow.

Sissy checked the wounded men in the office one final time, then climbed into a wagon. She wrapped her scarf around her head to keep out the cold. She had been at the mine for hours and was so tired she almost fell asleep the moment she sat down. But she knew Doc would need her to be alert.

After the long ride home, she went into the surgery. Greenie was helping Doc and looked relieved that Sissy was there. "I'll fix you coffee," Greenie said. Doc was treating the last miner she'd sent down, the man with the head injury.

"He's the final one. I took care of everyone else, and they're waiting for rides home," Sissy said.

"Nobody died?" Doc asked.

"No. We were lucky."

"Yes, we were," Doc said. The miner was sitting in a chair, and Doc helped him up. "You're going to be all right, but you take it easy. And no liquor." Doc turned to Sissy.

"Go see to Bert Alameda, the man you sent down with the injured leg. Check to see if he's still bleeding. I managed to save the leg for now, but we won't know for a few days whether he can keep it. He's in the spare room along with the two men I brought down with me. Mrs. Greenway set up cots for them."

Sissy checked on the miner and returned several minutes later. "No more bleeding for Mr. Alameda, and they're all sleeping. That's a good sign, isn't it?"

Doc nodded. "We'll keep them for a few days." He looked at her. "It's been a long day. You go lie down, now."

As Sissy started for the door, Doc said, "Oh, Sis?" Sissy stopped and turned back to her father. "You did a good job up there. I'm proud of you."

Sissy smiled as she thought, *That's the best compliment you've ever paid me, Papa.*

As tired as she was, Sissy was too excited to go to bed. She pushed back the curtain in the parlor and saw that the snow had stopped. So she put on her boots and coat, thinking she would tramp up to her aspen grove, but she hadn't gone far when she realized the snow was too deep to make it up the mountain. She brushed snow off a rock outcropping and sat down there instead. Despite her mittens and heavy stockings, her fingers and toes tingled. Her cheeks hurt from the cold. Still, she didn't leave the rock.

She thought about the day. Doc had trusted her to examine and treat the miners on her own. He had said he was proud of her. She looked out over the snow gleaming in the moonlight. The jack pines sent long, dark shadows across the whiteness. Sissy picked up a stick and swished it through the snow, leaving deep cuts.

"I did it, Jack," she whispered. "I was just like Papa, helping people who were hurt. It's a good feeling. Do *you* think I could be a doctor?"

The night was silent except for the muffled noise coming from the town. Sissy sat for a long time, looking out at the sky. Then, far up, she saw a star fall.

26

Late one night in early May, a man came to the Carlson house to fetch Doc. He said there'd been an accident down the valley in the town of Drunken Jack. A wagon had overturned, and two men were injured. They were close to death.

"Want me to come with you?" Sissy asked. She stood in the surgery in her nightgown as Doc collected his things.

"You go back to bed. Don't worry if I'm gone for a day or two," Doc told her. "After the job you did at the Yellowcat last month, I know you can handle scrapes and bruises. For anything more serious, do what you can and tell folks I'll take care of them as soon as I get back."

"Yes, sir." After the mine accident, she knew Doc had more confidence in her. She watched him climb into the man's wagon, which rattled off into the dark.

Sissy stood in the doorway, listening to the night sounds of Tenmile. She heard the noise of the Yellowcat and the thumping of the mill. Up on the mountain, voices rose as men came off shift and made their way down the slope. A piano banged in one of the saloons that was open day and night. The sound she liked best was that of the wind blowing through the jack pines and the new leaves of the aspen trees. It was truly spring, and the air was warmer now. Soon the hummingbirds would come. Sissy waited until she couldn't hear the wagon anymore. Then she went back to bed.

When she awoke, she dressed and went into the kitchen. Greenie was fixing bacon and flapjacks. "Sit you down. There's sorghum on the table," the housekeeper said. "Doc's not partial to flapjacks. I figured since it's just me and you, I'd fix them."

Sissy grinned. "Maybe Papa should go away more often."

The two sat down and were just starting to eat when someone knocked on the back door. Greenie was startled.

"I hope it's nothing serious. What would we tell them?" She went to the door and opened it.

A young girl stood there. At first, Sissy didn't recognize her in the dim dawn light, but Greenie did. "Why, little Sarah Washington! You come right in. Don't stand there in the cold." Then Sissy remembered the girl from the cabin in the mountains. Her father had had the ague in the fall.

Sarah came inside and stood next to the stove. She wasn't wearing a coat and shivered as she placed one bare foot on top of the other. Sissy wondered if she even owned shoes.

"Is your father sick again?" she asked.

Sarah shook her head. "Pa's fine." She stared at the food on the table.

Greenie spoke up. "You just sit yourself here. You can have some breakfast while you tell us what's wrong."

The little girl looked at Sissy for permission. Sissy nodded. Sarah went to the table and sat down, taking a flapjack in her hand. She poured sorghum over it, then shoved it into her mouth and licked her hand.

"You eat the rest of them," Greenie told her. Sarah picked up a second one and began eating it.

Then she said with her mouth full, "Ma's baby's coming."

"Your ma's having a baby?" Sissy asked. "When?"

"Right now. Pa says he don't know what to do. He ain't never birthed a baby before. He's scared." Sarah spotted the bacon and took a piece. "Ma's head is vexed, just like Pa's was when he was sick, and she's hollering. Water's running down her face something bad. Pa says get Doc."

"Doctor Carlson isn't here. He left this morning to go down valley. He might not be back for a couple of days," Greenie said.

Sarah looked puzzled. "We don't know no Doc Carlson. Pa says fetch Doc Sissy."

Sissy and Greenie stared at each other. "Heaven's mercy!" Greenie said. "I told Doc that's what they're calling you up at the Cat now."

"I'm not a doctor," Sissy told the little girl.

"You fixed up Pa right good."

"But he wasn't having a baby." Sissy turned to Greenie. "Willow Louise ought to wait for Papa."

"You know as well as I do that babies don't wait. If she's already having pains, this one's likely to come before Doc gets back."

"But—"

"Oh, for goodness' sake, Sissy, you know more about delivering babies than any woman on the Tenmile," Greenie told her. "You've helped your papa deliver a dozen of them."

Greenie was right. Still, Sissy thought, *I only helped. I never delivered one by myself.*

"You better hurry. Ma's hurting," Sarah said. She had finished the flapjacks. She reached out a sticky hand. "Come on, Doc Sissy."

Sissy turned to Greenie. "I don't know . . ."

"You go get what you need, *Doc* Sissy," Greenie said, smiling. "I'll write a note for Doc Carlson to come along as soon as he gets back. I'll leave directions. Where are you living, child? You're not up in that cabin still, are you?"

"We come down to Chicken Flats for the winter. Pa worked at the mill. But he said when spring come, he'd go back to prospecting. So we're up the mountain in the cabin again."

Sissy hurried into the surgery. Doc had taken his medical bag, so she packed what she needed in a sugar sack. Greenie put together a basket of food while Sarah ate the last of the bacon. Then the three set out on the long walk up the mountain.

The sun had reached the mountainside. Still, it was chilly. Sissy wondered how Sarah could walk barefoot across the cold earth. Dew covered the pinecones and the long, thin pine needles scattered about. A few wildflowers peeked out from behind rocks and stumps. If she hadn't been in such a hurry, Sissy would have picked a bouquet of them for Willow Louise.

Sarah bounded up the mountain like a little fawn. Sissy followed as fast as she could, and Greenie puffed along after them. She stopped for a moment to catch her breath. "You go on. I'll be right behind you," she said.

Sissy didn't want to leave her, but she was anxious to reach Willow Louise. "Are you sure?" Greenie waved her along.

When she heard a cry, Sissy began to run until the cabin came into view. The door was open. Sissy followed Sarah inside. There was still no bed. Willow Louise lay on a pallet on the floor. Eual Washington was hovering over her. He looked up. "Doc's here," he told his wife.

Sissy didn't feel like a doctor. She knew Doc couldn't be there, but she desperately wished he was. She would be his assistant. *What if something goes wrong?* Sissy asked herself. *Will I know what to do? What if the baby dies, or Willow*

Louise? It will be my fault. She almost wished the baby had been born before she'd gotten there.

For a moment, she stood rooted to the dirt floor. She couldn't move. Then Willow Louise reached out her hand. "Thanks, Doc," she said.

Greenie came into the cabin. "Bless my soul! We got here in time. You're in good hands with Doc Sissy. Now you tell us what to do, Doc." She nudged Sissy forward.

Sissy swallowed, then straightened her back. She reminded herself that she'd held her own during the Yellowcat disaster. Moreover, she'd helped her father deliver lots of babies. She knew how to do it. Willow Louise needed her. Sissy couldn't just stand there like a stump.

She turned to Eual. "We'll need hot water."

"Done it. I bucketed the water and put it on the fire, too." He pointed to the fireplace, where a kettle of water sat on a trivet.

Sissy told him to pour water into a basin for her. She washed her hands. Then she examined Willow Louise.

"Just in time," she told Greenie. "The baby's crowning. I can see the top of its head." She looked around and spotted a stick leaning against the wall. "Break off a piece of that stick.

Willow Louise can bite down on it when the pain comes. That way she won't bite her tongue."

Greenie reached for the stick, but Eual grabbed it away from her. "Don't you touch that. It's my dowsing stick. Sarah, you find a stick for your ma."

Sarah hurried to the table and picked up her mother's stirring stick.

"It's what?" Sissy asked, pausing in her examination.

"A dowsing stick. It's forked, see?" Greenie explained. "You hold it in both hands and point the end at the ground. Mostly it's used to find water. When the end starts to shiver and shake, it means there's water below. Some believe it can find gold, too."

Sissy had never heard of such a thing, but she didn't have time to think about it. She knelt on the pallet beside Willow Louise.

Sarah handed her mother the stirring stick. Willow Louise put it between her teeth.

"When you feel a pain, you bite down on that stick. Then you push," Sissy said. "A few more pains, and you'll push that baby right out."

"She gonna be all right?" Eual asked.

"You bet she is," Sissy said. She tried to sound like Doc when he reassured patients they would be fine. As she did so, she felt a surge of confidence. Of course Willow Louise would be all right. Women delivered babies all the time. Sissy had seen many babies born with not a single problem.

Sarah crept close to her mother. She looked frightened. Sissy thought she needed something to do. "Will you get a wet cloth and wipe your mother's head?" Sissy asked her.

Willow Louise twisted and cried out as a pain hit her. She lay with her knees in the air. Sissy positioned herself between them.

"Push!" Sissy said. Willow Louise pushed, and the baby's head emerged. "That's good, Willow Louise. Now let out little puffs like you're blowing out the lamp." Sissy waited until there was another pain and Willow Louise groaned. "Once more. Push!" Willow Louise did as she was told. She reached out and gripped Sarah's hand.

"One last time," Sissy said. Willow Louise gave a final push, and moments later, Sissy was holding the newborn in her hands.

"A boy!" Eual shouted.

Sissy sighed with relief. The baby looked fine. She tied

off the umbilical cord and cut it with a knife. She handed the baby to Greenie. Then Sissy delivered the placenta. When she was finished, Sissy used her sleeve to wipe the perspiration from her face.

"You did good, real good, Doc Sissy," Greenie said, beaming at the infant. He had black eyes as tiny as shoe buttons and hair sticking out in all directions. His ears stuck out, too. His legs were as thick and lumpy as stone fence posts. "Why, bless my soul, he's God's perfect child," Greenie said.

She washed the baby and wrapped him in a flannel blanket she had set near the fire to warm. Greenie cooed at the baby and hummed a little song. Then she stopped suddenly. Sissy was tending Willow Louise and turned around, alarmed.

"Is he all right?" she asked.

"I don't know," Greenie replied.

"What's wrong?"

"He doesn't seem to be breathing." Greenie held out the baby.

"What?" Willow Louise asked, trying to sit up. Eual went to Greenie and stared at the baby.

Sissy took the infant from her. His eyes were now closed.

Greenie was right. The baby was still. Too still. Sissy laid him over one arm and patted his back, but he didn't draw a breath. "What should I do?" she asked.

Greenie shook her head, a helpless look on her face. Eual went to Willow Louise and took her hand. "Doc Sissy will fix him," he said, trying to reassure his wife. He looked up at Sissy, waiting for her to agree with him.

Sissy tried to remember if this had ever happened when she assisted her father, but she couldn't recall a single time. Something was wrong with the baby, and Doc wasn't there to help. She needed to figure this out on her own. She checked the baby's mouth to see if anything was stuck in it. His mouth was clear.

Perspiration ran down her face. Sissy wanted to cry, but she couldn't, not now. The baby's life was in her hands. She wished she knew what to do. Then she remembered Doc had once said that, when everything failed, you should do what seemed natural.

Sissy sat down on a stump near the fire and put the baby on her lap. She stretched out her legs so that the baby's body sloped downward, his head near her knees. She gently began to massage the tiny child's stomach.

"Live, baby, live!" she whispered. She forgot there was anyone else in the room as she concentrated on the boy. Greenie and Eual and Sarah were silent as they watched her. Willow Louise's eyes were closed. She was praying.

"Please, baby," Sissy whispered, still stroking the tiny tummy.

Suddenly, the infant gasped. He opened his shoe-button eyes and looked up. Sissy knew newborn babies didn't see very well. Still, she was sure he was looking right at her. The baby began to wail.

Eual slapped his leg. Willow Louise grinned at Greenie. Sarah clapped her hands.

"You did it!" Greenie said. "You did it, Doc Sissy!"

She had done it! Sissy was so happy she wanted to hug herself. She'd come through when Willow Louise and Eual and Sarah—and the baby—needed her.

Later, Willow Louise slept on a fresh quilt Greenie had laid on the pallet. Sarah held the baby boy in her arms. Eual patted his downy hair. "It's fine as frog's hair," he said.

Greenie bustled around the cabin, gathering up old quilts and dirty clothes. She promised to wash them and bring them back. Next, she grabbed her basket. She removed part of a ham, a loaf of bread, and a jar of pickles and set them on the table.

"That should hold you for a while. I'll bring biscuits and fried chicken next time I come." She looked around the cabin for another quilt and put it over Willow Louise.

Willow Louise woke, reached for the baby, and ran her finger over his forehead. "Little bitsy thing. What are we going to call our boy?"

Eual turned and stared at his dowsing stick. "I been hunting all over for gold up here, and I think I just found it. Ain't nothing that shines as bright as our boy. I expect we should call him Goldie."

Sissy waited until Goldie had been fed and was sleeping. The boy had nursed properly, and his breathing was normal. She gently checked him over one more time to make sure he was doing well. Then she picked up her things. She said she or Doc Carlson would be back the next day to see if both mother and baby were all right. "You send Sarah for me if you need me," she said. Then she and Greenie started for the door.

"Tap 'er light, now," Greenie called.

Early the next morning, Sissy went out to the woodpile to bring in kindling for the cookstove. On top of the pile was a forked stick. The wood looked polished and shone like amber in the sunlight. Sissy picked it up and took it inside. "Look what I found," she said. She held up the stick so Greenie could see it.

"It's Eual's dowsing stick," Greenie said. She took the stick from Sissy and rubbed her hands over the smooth wood.

"Why did he leave it here? Do you think he's given up looking for gold?" Sissy asked.

"I think it means he's already found it," Greenie replied. "This stick is the most valuable thing he has. Giving it to you is his way of paying you for delivering Goldie. I'd say you've been paid in full."

27

DOC DIDN'T RETURN HOME UNTIL the afternoon. Sissy could hardly wait. She checked the window each time she heard horses pass by. When Doc finally stepped down from the wagon, Sissy ran out of the house and shouted, "Papa, I delivered a baby!" She grinned at him.

"What?" Doc looked tired and like he wasn't paying much attention.

"A baby. I delivered a baby."

"What? Whose baby?" Doc gave her a sharp look.

"Willow Louise. She lives up the mountain. Her husband was the one with the ague."

Greenie came outside and took Doc's medical bag from him. "She did an awful good job of it, Doc. You'd have been proud of her."

"The woman came here, did she?" he asked. "You delivered the baby in the surgery?"

"No, she sent her girl, Sarah, to fetch us. We went to their cabin. The baby was born there," Sissy said. "I went up to check on him this morning, and everything's fine."

Doc stared at her. "You should have waited for me, Sis."

"We couldn't. She needed us. The baby was born yesterday. You weren't here."

Doc blew out his breath. "I don't know. What if something had gone wrong? What would you have done?"

"Something did go wrong," Greenie said. "It was the darndest thing, Doc. That baby stopped breathing, and Sissy brought him back to life. I don't know how she did it, but your daughter performed a miracle. I'd say she did as fine a job as you ever could."

"What happened? What'd you do, Sis?"

Sissy told him how she'd laid Goldie on her legs with his head down and massaged his stomach.

Doc considered her reply. "Why'd you do that?"

"I don't know, Papa. You said once that when you're stumped, you should do what feels natural. Holding that baby in my lap and rubbing his tummy just seemed like the right thing to do, and it worked."

"You have a good mind," Doc said. "You know, Sis, that's what Mr. Gilpin told me after he watched you care for the miners. You examined the injured and decided which ones to send to me. Then you sewed up cuts and checked for concussions. And during it all, according to Mr. Gilpin, you were the coolest-headed person up there. He told me you have a good heart, too. Mr. Gilpin believes you ought to study medicine. He even said he might see his way clear to helping you, if you thought you would come back to Tenmile afterward."

Sissy looked at her father in shock. "Really, Papa?"

Doc nodded.

"I liked caring for those men and for Willow Louise," Sissy said.

"Caring for people is important up here in Tenmile. With life so hard, folks need to know someone is on their side. And with what you just told me about Willow Louise's baby . . . well, you've got the right instincts for treating patients. But then, I've known that all along."

Sissy was shocked. "You have?"

Doc nodded. He looked out over the valley at the Yellowcat, where men were working, then down at Chicken Flats.

"I've tried to discourage you from a career in medicine. That's because I know it's a hard life, and even harder for a woman. But in fact, I've thought for a long time that you have what it takes to be a wonderful nurse. Now I'm sure of it."

Sissy was flustered and didn't know what to say, but Greenie did.

"You got that right, Doc. Sissy could be a nurse or more. You know there's a medical school for women down in Boulder? I checked."

Doc gave her a stern look. "Yes, you already told me that. More than once." He turned to Sissy. "I know about that tin can you keep your money in, too. You thought it was a secret. I think you can put that away."

It was late afternoon as Sissy walked up the mountain. The jack pines sent long shadows across the trail. The sun came through in patches, making the pale green leaves of the aspen trees shimmer. Startled by her intrusion, a bird as blue as the sky flew up in front of Sissy. She stopped in her special place and sat down on the fallen log. The squirrel ran up a tree, *tsk-tsk*ing at her.

"Tired?" asked Greenie.

Sissy was startled. She hadn't known Greenie was following her. She reached out her hand, and Greenie took it as she sat down beside Sissy.

"You know I wouldn't even be thinking about a career if it wasn't for you," Sissy said. "Thank you, Greenie."

Greenie didn't respond but used her sleeve to wipe her eyes. She squeezed Sissy's hand. "You're not dreaming about being a nurse, are you?" the woman asked. "You want to be a doctor."

Sissy had been watching the squirrel. Now she turned to Greenie and grinned.

"You don't have to tell Doc just now," Greenie said. "We'll wait and see what happens."

Sissy nodded, then turned to stare out over Tenmile. She

could see the smoke and hear the faint sounds of the mine and mill. She glanced over at the Gilpin mansion shining in the sun. Then she looked down at Chicken Flats. Those were her people—hers and Doc's and Greenie's. They needed Doc and Greenie, and someday they would need her, too.

In the past year, she had faced challenges and overcome them. She'd stepped in to treat the miners at the Yellowcat when they'd needed her. She'd kept up Nelle's and Jack's hopes when things had been dismal. Sissy missed her friends and always would, but they were with her in spirit. She thought of Jack and how he had wanted her to go on. She still mourned his death, but she understood now that loss and sadness were part of life. So was the joy of birth. Willow Louise's baby had lived because of her.

For a long time, she'd wanted to leave Tenmile, but now Sissy knew it was her home. It was where she was needed, where she should be, where she *wanted* to be.

Sissy stood and reached down to pull Greenie up, and the two walked hand in hand down the mountain to her town—to Tenmile.

FROM *the* AUTHOR

"Life was so hard on the Tenmile. Was it that hard in other places?" Sissy asks herself in *Tenmile*.

Indeed it was. Conditions in Colorado's early gold and silver mining towns were difficult, especially for women. Men joined the gold rush in the 1860s and 1870s, hoping to strike it rich. For women, however, westering often meant leaving behind the things they cared about most. They exchanged friends and family and the comforts of home for the dangers of wild mining camps. They lived in tents and log cabins set on muddy, garbage-strewn streets. Food was unsanitary and hygiene poor. There were plenty of gamblers and confidence men, but not many teachers, preachers, or doctors.

By the 1880s, when *Tenmile* takes place, towns had been established with churches and schools, stores, and services. There were theaters and restaurants that served everything from pork chop sandwiches to East Coast oysters. Townspeople never knew when they might glimpse a national politician, a mining magnate, or a world-famous celebrity. The rich wore finery and jewels and lived in expensive houses.

But everyday workers and their families still lived in crowded shacks. By then, most of the men who went west were not prospectors looking for gold and silver but blue-collar workers hoping for jobs. Mining was dangerous. Working underground, men might be permanently injured or killed in accidents. Damp conditions in the mines made it easier for workers to develop the "miner's puff"—tuberculosis—which they sometimes spread to their wives and children. Freezing winters, as well as smoke from mines and smelters—which made it difficult to see even in the daytime—meant colds and pneumonia and other medical problems.

Life was especially hard for women. Because wages in the mines were low, wives took in laundry or did mending or cared for boarders to make ends meet. When a man was injured or sickened or died, his wife had to find employment. If she was educated, she could teach school, but few women were qualified. Many, in fact, were illiterate or were immigrants who barely spoke English. That left backbreaking domestic work, for which they might be paid merely a bucket of coal or an old shirt. Children often quit school to help support their families.

Some boys dreamed of going to college, but few made it, and even fewer girls continued their educations beyond high school. Attending college took determination, hard work, and luck. And even if a girl managed to graduate, she almost never joined a profession. Most colleges forbade women from taking classes in law or medicine. (Harvard Medical School didn't admit women until 1945.)

Nelly Mayo, the first woman to graduate from the University of Colorado School of Medicine, didn't obtain her degree until 1891. Dr. Mayo was likely born in the mid-1860s, which made her close to Sissy's age. Sissy and Nelly might have attended classes together, studied together, and helped each other fight discrimination. I like to think that Sissy was just a year behind her friend Nelly at school. That would make Sissy the second woman to graduate from the University of Colorado School of Medicine. Doc would have been so proud, and both he and Greenie would have attended graduation to cheer her on.

So many people helped me with *Tenmile*. Barb McNally, senior children's editor at Sleeping Bear Press, brought the book together. I couldn't have completed it without her vision and hard work. I'm indebted to Dr. Carl Bartecchi, Dr. Stanley Kerstein, and Marsha Merry for sharing their medical knowledge. Danielle Egan-Miller, my agent at Browne & Miller Literary Associates, is always there when I need her. And then there is my wonderful family—Bob, Dana, Kendal, Lloyd, and especially Forrest. You're the reason I wrote *Tenmile*, Forrest.

SANDRA DALLAS

Sandra Dallas is the *New York Times*-bestselling author of the middle-grade novels *Hardscrabble, The Quilt Walk, Red Berries, White Clouds, Blue Sky,* and *Someplace to Call Home.* A member of the Colorado Authors' Hall of Fame, she is the author of ten nonfiction books and seventeen adult novels, including *The Last Midwife, Prayers for Sale, The Diary of Mattie Spenser, The Persian Pickle Club,* and *Little Souls.* A former Denver bureau chief for *Business Week* magazine, she is the recipient of three National Cowboy & Western Heritage Museum Wrangler awards, four Western Writers of America Spur Awards, and six Women Writing the West WILLA Awards. She lives in Denver and Georgetown, Colorado. Visit her at www.sandradallas.com.

MORE MIDDLE-GRADE OFFERINGS FROM SANDRA DALLAS

SOMEPLACE TO CALL HOME
In 1933, three orphaned siblings find themselves in a small Kansas town, where they are met with suspicion and hostility. A timely story of young people searching for a home and a better way of life.

HARDSCRABBLE
In 1910, after losing their farm in Iowa, twelve-year-old Belle Martin and her family move to Colorado to start over as homesteaders. Do the Martins have what it takes to thrive in their new prairie life?

THE QUILT WALK
A young girl's western journey is chronicled in a historical fiction offering for middle-grade readers.

RED BERRIES WHITE CLOUDS BLUE SKY
In this moving story, a young girl overcomes the prejudices and suspicions of World War II while finding hope in the unlikeliest of places.